SEAL'S SUNSHINE (SPECIAL FORCES: OPERATION ALPHA)

BLACK EAGLE TEAM 2

LYNNE ST. JAMES

Cover by Lori Jackson Designs
Created in the United States

Dear Readers,

Welcome to the Special Forces: Operation Alpha Fan-Fiction world!

If you are new to this amazing world, in a nutshell the author wrote a story using one or more of my characters in it. Sometimes that character has a major role in the story, and other times they are only mentioned briefly. This is perfectly legal and allowable because they are going through Aces Press to publish the story.

This book is entirely the work of the author who wrote it. While I might have assisted with brainstorming and other ideas about which of my characters to use, I didn't have any part in the process or writing or editing the story.

I'm proud and excited that so many authors loved my characters enough that they wanted to write them into their own story. Thank you for supporting them, and me!

READ ON!

Xoxo

Susan Stoker

NOTE TO READERS

I can't thank Susan Stoker enough for letting me use her characters to help me tell my stories. I love her books and being able to include them in my books is like extra toppings on my ice cream. Even better, is the opportunity to share my books with you. Susan is an amazing author and her friendship and support mean so much.

In ***SEAL's Sunshine***, I've included John "Tex" Keegan in my story. I have done my best to keep him true to Susan's vision, but I may have taken certain allowances for my story.

I hope you enjoy ***SEAL's Sunshine***. Remember, the best way to thank an author is to leave a review.

Lynne

DEDICATION

For all the spouses and families who are patiently waiting for their soldiers to return home.

As always, for T.S., my real life hero. I love you!

ACKNOWLEDGMENTS

Writing this book was harder than usual for many reasons, but these women and their incredible support and encouragement kept me going. I can't thank you enough Marcia Bucktin, Christine Evans, and Dawn Montgomery. You are the best!

A huge thank you to Karen DiGaetano for being a kicka$$ beta reader and keeping me honest!

CHAPTER 1

"I CAN'T WAIT TO GET OUT OF THIS HELL HOLE. This deployment has sucked," Cameron "Cam" Patterson said as he packed his gear and fed Halo, his K-9 teammate. After a three-month deployment to Bagram Air Force Base in Afghanistan, he was more than ready to go home, especially since his Sunshine was waiting for him.

"What? Are you're tired of sand in every crevice of your body?" Rafe asked as he loaded his pack.

"No shit. Every time we're here it seems worse."

"You're lucky, kid. Wait until you're caught in a haboob. Then you can complain about it," Rafe said. He was their second in command. "But I have to agree, this deployment was boring as fuck. Home sounds great right now."

"He's just in a hurry to get back to see his woman for a little batter-dipping the corndog," Drew "Murph" Murphy, sniper and overall pain in the ass, commented as he came in from the showers.

Cam was the youngest and newest member of the Black Eagle team. He'd been lucky when Jake Warner, their master chief, had picked him from the group of frogmen that had gotten through BUD/S almost four years ago. Sure, he took a lot of shit from them, but he had no doubt they had his six, and he sure as hell had theirs. It'd been a bonus to be Halo's K-9 handler too. The large German shepherd was an excellent soldier and made a great companion when they were home.

Ignoring Murph's comment about Miranda, he'd just finished packing his gear when the door opened and Jake entered with their CIA liaison, Bill Lynch following close behind.

"Bad news, jokers, we're not leaving quite yet."

"Are you fucking kidding me?" Cam said before he could stop himself. It had been hard being away this time, but since Tex had given him a tracker to put on Miranda's phone, at least he knew she was safe. It was the same type that Meghan, Rafe's girlfriend, had on her phone. It had helped them find her when she'd been taken by the Taliban. John "Tex" Keegan was an ex-

SEAL and now used his incredible computer skills to help them. Now he was like an extended member of the team.

Jake gave him the 'watch it' look before continuing. "Red Falcon Team is delayed on another mission. We're the only team available and this comes from the top of the food chain. Captain wants us in the TOC asap."

"Aww fuck. We were so close to a clean getaway," Ryan McLaughlin, the team medic said. "I swear it's a conspiracy."

"Conspiracy my ass," Murph said. "It's payback for going off-book when we rescued Rafe's woman."

"Enough bitching. It's like being with a group of old women. We have work to do," Jake said in a "don't fuck with me" tone. Hearing that meant only one thing, shit was about to hit the fan.

The team assembled in the TOC and waited for Captain Tony Knox to brief them on the mission that stood between them and a flight home. As happy as Cam was to do something other than training, the timing sucked. Even if he didn't want to admit it to the guys, he was anxious to get home since Miranda flying in to stay with him for a week.

She'd been recovering from her abduction when he'd had to deploy, but they had managed a few dates before he left, and lots of Skype calls since. There had been something that had clicked when he saw her. She'd gone through hell at the hands of the Taliban and had kept it together, been so strong. Even covered in bruises, she'd taken his breath away. Daydreaming about her was pretty much constant when he wasn't on maneuvers and it got him into trouble a few times.

The door opened admitting the captain and the colonel. If the colonel was part of the briefing, they were most likely walking into a shitshow of epic proportions. It took that kind of a mission for him to show up in the TOC.

"I know you are ready to head home, but we get to keep you for a while longer," the colonel said as he met each of their eyes. It was as if he was assessing their readiness. They were SEALs and always ready. "We have a delicate situation. The CIA has picked up chatter about an impending attack in Saudi Arabia and you're the only spec ops team who is close enough to get there in time to neutralize the situation."

"We'll do whatever it takes, Sir," Jake responded. "What's the mission?"

"Protecting POTUS. He's flying in for negotiations with the Saudis. It's been kept under wraps, but the threat was deemed credible. No one was supposed to know about this trip and that opens up other issues, but they aren't your problem. Your mission is to eliminate the threat. You are standing between evil and the leader of the free world. Don't fuck up."

As per his usual, he dropped his intel bomb and departed, leaving the captain and Lynch to fill in the blanks. No wonder Jake looked pissed off when he'd come to get them.

"I know you have a lot of questions, but we'll have to address them on the plane. Get your gear. Wheels up in ten."

Cam caught Jake and Rafe as they exchanged glances and it made the hair on the back of his neck tingle. Even though it was POTUS, no one had explained the credible threat. When it involved the President of the United States, a Charlie Foxtrot aka cluster fuck was guaranteed.

On the transport with time to spare, they stowed their gear. Then he put food and water dishes down for Halo and joined the team where they had gathered for the briefing. It wasn't normal protocol, but there was a leak and until they knew where it was from, the plane was one of the more secure areas.

"What's up, boss?" Murph asked, his impatience evident. He was like an older brother and a black-sheep merged into one. If you asked who on the Black Eagle Team caused the most eye rolls, the answer was always Murph.

"Is POTUS on site?" Rafe asked.

"No, he's landing at zero nine hundred. We'll

have three and a half hours once we land to verify, find, and eliminate the threat."

"Piece of cake," Murph said, which earned him a side eye from the captain. Cam wondered if he'd ever learn to keep his fucking trap shut at times like this.

"What do we know?" Cam asked. They needed the intel available to come up with their plan. Although knowing Jake, if he'd made a plan that would be close to perfect already.

Captain Knox signaled Lynch to take over. "The chatter we picked up indicates a plan to blow up Air Force One as soon as it lands with POTUS on board. And before you ask, yes, it's credible intel."

"Do you know who's behind it? What else do we know?" Rafe asked, his expression grim, which mirrored everyone else's on the team. As usual, they were short on intel and time to figure it out.

"Not much. It appears to be an offshoot of ISIS that has joined up with Al-Qaeda.

"Fuck, this is a thing now?" Murph asked.

"Yeah, we've been picking up chatter about this partnership for the last few months. But this is the first intel we've got that is verified."

"Do we have any idea who's involved? Names? Locations? Anything? You're not giving us much to go on and we're stuck on this plane for two and a half hours," Jake asked, shooting questions one after another at Lynch.

"I know it sucks. But we do know one name, and it's familiar to you too. Azfaar."

"What the ever living fuck? How did he go from the Taliban to ISIS and Al-Qaeda?"

"Apparently, he took the missionary group without approval from his superiors. When it turned into a shit show, he had the choice to disappear or die. He went running to the biggest rats for protection and now he has an ax to grind."

"Is that why he's going after POTUS?"

"It's how he sold it to his new friends. But we think his real target is a smaller fish—Senator Stanhope. But Stanhope wouldn't have made a big enough impact for them to agree. Taking out POTUS would put them in the upper echelon of all the terrorist groups. They'd be back in the game with no shortage of money and supporters." Lynch spread out a map of the area around the airfield.

"Any indication where they might be holed up?" Jake asked.

"Not yet. I have my contacts working on it, but I may not hear anything else until we land."

"Okay, you heard him. Be prepared to hit the ground running. The clock is ticking gentlemen and the fate of the free world depends on us and we'll have a little over three hours to pull it off," Captain Knox said.

It was way over the top even for the captain and sounded like a fucking recruitment commercial, but when Cam thought about it, he was right. If Azfaar pulled this off, it would set off a string of events that would change the world.

"One other thing, other than the people you're looking at, no one else has been briefed. We don't know who can be trusted after the leak. Until this threat is diffused, we are on our own."

"Copy that."

"Get some rest. Wheels down in just over an hour," the captain said as he and Lynch walked toward the front of the plane. It wouldn't surprise Cam if there was information they'd held back. It wouldn't be the first time and definitely not the last. But they would do whatever it took to complete their mission.

"So it looks like Miranda's father is the real target. Cam, can you keep your head in the game?"

"Fuck, seriously, Jake? Would you ask Rafe or Murph? Rafe has just as much invested in taking out Azfaar as I do. I'm a SEAL, the job is first always."

"Just checking, and I've already asked Rafe. So get that chip off your shoulder. I need to make sure everyone's head is where it needs to be." It was his job. Cam understood but it still rubbed him the wrong way. Luckily, Jake didn't ask for specifics, because he'd be lying if he didn't admit to the desire to tear Azfaar's head off with his bare hands.

~

It was a beautiful sunny morning in Atlanta, and Miranda Stanhope was taking advantage of the peace and quiet by having her coffee in the backyard. The garden was filled with color, the azaleas were covered in pink and red blooms. The peonies and roses were also loaded with colorful flowers. The fountain in the corner gurgled and Miranda sighed with pleasure as she sipped from her mug. This was her favorite time of day. Her mother was still asleep, her father was away on a trip, and she had the little slice of heaven all to herself.

Shifting in her chair to alleviate the residual pain in her side from her broken ribs at the hands of the Taliban, she closed her eyes and tried to clear her mind. Inhaling the scents of the flowers helped push away the sudden fear she was being watched. The backyard was secluded and surrounded by a tall brick wall. It had to be her imagination, or PTSD if she listened to Cam, or Charlie, one of the other missionaries who'd been abducted. Either way, it didn't make it any easier living with the pain. The angry scars that covered both of her legs from her thighs to her knees were another constant reminder of her time in captivity.

Her father said it was common for not just the military but also those who'd been in traumatic situations. One thing they all suggested was for her to talk to a professional to help her work through her issues. She'd resisted. Unable to remember everything that happened, she'd still experienced nightmares and woke up drenched in sweat and shaking more times than not.

Eventually, she and Charlie talked, and it had helped a bit. The nightmares didn't come every night now, although they still popped up at least once a week. More when she was stressed.

Charlie's experience hadn't been the same. She'd been separated from the main group and when they'd found out she was a senator's daughter. But he'd almost lost his sister, Meghan when she'd tried to help rescue them and almost died in the process.

The Deliver Hope Ministries had been working hard to gather the resources to send another group to finish what they'd started. Charlie volunteered to lead the group, but most of the others had bowed out. Not that she blamed them, it was a terrifying trip and not an experience she wanted to repeat either. But she felt obligated to help the women. Even though going back was the last thing Miranda wanted, she knew how much they needed the school built and teachers brought in. Charlie had been thrilled when she told him she'd go with him, but she'd held off telling Cam so far.

It had been over three months since she'd seen him, and she'd still been using crutches. There had been something between them from the first moment she'd seen him. He'd been part of the SEAL team who'd rescued her, and she'd be grateful forever, but with Cam, it was more than just gratitude. In the beginning, she told herself it was just hero worship but the more time they spent together the more she realized it was different. He was special in a way she hadn't felt about anyone before.

Dating a Navy SEAL had its drawbacks, mostly since she never knew when they'd have a mission. When he was gone she never knew where he was or when he'd be back. It was a bit easier for her since her father worked for the CIA before he retired and entered politics. Growing up, she'd known he traveled a lot but not what he did. It wasn't until he retired that she found out. Secrecy had always been part of her life.

Just thinking about Cam made her smile. And Halo. She loved that dog. He'd been the first one to reach her in the cave and then helped to keep her calm. But it was Cam's kind blue eyes that had erased the fear. The other SEAL, Ryan, took care of her injuries, but Cam held her hand to make sure she'd stayed calm. After they left her at Bagram with the medical staff, she thought she'd never see any of them again.

Instead, he'd checked on her more than once before they sent her to Germany for further treatment. Then after they got back to the states he'd taken her out a few times, including to Meghan and Rafe's, one of the other SEAL team members, for their housewarming party. It was awkward at first, but they were so nice, like a huge family of teddy bears, not that she'd ever say it to their faces. Meghan and her friend Chrissy were great too and knowing Meghan had been through a lot of the same treatment at the hands of the Taliban, made it easier.

It was no wonder she was up early, today was extra special. Cam was due back from his three-month deployment, and she was flying to Norfolk to stay with him for a week. It was going to be her first time there. So far he'd come to Atlanta to stay with her, under the watchful eye of her mother.

Rafe's girlfriend Meghan was supposed to pick her up at the airport since she was due in before the guys landed. Then she'd stay with her until Cam came for her. She really liked him and was nervous she'd do something to ruin it. But if there was one thing she learned it was that if you wanted something you needed to go after it.

"Miranda, honey, are you packed?"

"Yes, Mom. I packed last night. I just have to shower and get dressed."

Mrs. Cherise Stanhope, ex-socialite, and still one of the most beautiful women Miranda had ever seen, strolled onto the patio with her morning juice concoction in a crystal glass.

"I don't know how you drink that. It looks disgusting."

"It keeps me healthy, and it would be good for you to have too instead of that coffee all the time. Besides, what's wrong with green? It's a beautiful color. You know, I've even got your dad drinking them now."

"Ugh. You won't be converting me anytime soon so don't even try. I love my coffee too much."

"A little juicing couldn't hurt. Especially since you're still healing from that ordeal."

"I wouldn't call it an ordeal, and I'm healed, just have to keep up the exercises."

Cherise sighed as she pinched off a couple of the dying flowers on the potted plant next to her chair. "The gardener is slacking."

"You're too picky. The flower wasn't even dead yet, more like in the wilting stage. You're supposed to let them die then deadhead them."

"But then the whole plant looks untended."

Miranda rolled her eyes at her mother. She wasn't usually this ornery. It was because her dad was out of the country and she was leaving later. Her mother hated to be alone. Miranda had stayed close to home for college because of that. But she needed to make her own choices now. She was twenty-five years old and had her own life to live.

"Mom, it will be okay. Dad will be back in a few days and I'll call you as soon as I get to Meghan's house."

"Of course it'll be fine. I'm not worried." Her mom was a softy, but she hid it well. That was her good old southern charm, everything perfect on the outside, but if you were one of the privileged few, you'd see inside and get the real truth.

"I'm going to shower. Enjoy your drink," Miranda said with a chuckle. Then she came up behind Cherise and hugged her around the shoulders. "I love you, Mom."

Cherise patted her hand and smiled. "I love you too. I wish you wouldn't go. He could come here again."

"I know, but it's just for a week." Miranda had no intention of telling her that she was going on another trip for the Deliver Hope Ministries with Charlie. It could wait until she returned from

Cam's. No need to stress her out more than she already would be.

"Do you want me to drive you to the airport?"

"Nope," Miranda yelled over her shoulder. "I have an Uber coming to get me." Cherise said something but Miranda was out of range, and it was just as well. Instead of taking the elevator, she chose to make her way up the stairs, pushing herself and her recovery. She worked hard to get back to where she was before they'd beaten and tortured her almost to death and she was almost there.

The shower helped with her aches and eased some of the tension that had been with her since Afghanistan. More proof of PTSD according to Cam, and it might be, but she wasn't going to give in to it. After being released from PT, she was told she could ease back into her yoga routine. If anything would help her get rid of the tension, yoga would.

After applying some lipstick and mascara, she was ready to leave for the airport. Grabbing her overnight bag, she took the elevator this time, since the Atlanta-Hartsfield Airport was huge, and she never got lucky with the gate location.

After she gave her mom a hug and kiss goodbye, she was out the door before Cherise could try to convince her to stay home and have Cam come visit again. They'd already beaten that argument to death.

The closer she got to seeing Cam, the more her excitement bubbled inside. But knowing that by this time tomorrow she'd be with him, had her practically vibrating with happiness. It might be silly, but seeing his face made her happy and when they'd kissed the last few times they'd been together it had curled her toes. Since then she'd had quite a few restless nights and lots of cold showers when taking care of herself wasn't enough.

CHAPTER 2

THE FLIGHT TO NORFOLK WAS UNEVENTFUL after she gave in to the first class upgrade her mother had booked. Miranda needed to set some ground rules with her when she went back home. Grabbing the carry-on from the overhead, she waited as the other first-class passengers filed off the plane, and then headed for the waiting area. The walk wasn't too bad, and she saw Meghan almost as soon as she came through the sliding doors to the main terminal area.

"How was the flight?" Meghan asked as she hugged Miranda.

"Great. No turbulence and no chatty weird men. It doesn't get better than that."

"No shit, right? When I flew into Atlanta last time to visit my sister last month it was ridiculous. I ended up in a middle seat and the guy in the aisle kept hitting on me. Then the person in the window seat must have gotten up about twelve times to go to the bathroom. I was like seriously? It's a two-hour fight. Just stay in the fucking bathroom already."

"You need to let my mother make your reservations, then you'll end up in first class whether you want to or not."

"Why wouldn't you want to fly first class? I'd be all over that."

"I always feel like it's overkill. Especially on a short flight. Maybe I'm used to roughing since I've been on so many missionary trips."

"Speaking of trips, Charlie told me you guys are heading back in three months." They'd chatted as Meghan led the way to her car.

"Yeah, I haven't told my parents yet. I figured I'd wait until it got closer. I know they're going to freak out. But it's my job—at least for now."

"I'm sure they'll understand."

"Maybe my dad, but not my mother. She was freaking out about me coming here. It always was a problem, but it's gotten a million times worse since Afghanistan."

"You're her baby, an only child, right?"

"Yeah. I know she loves me and is just trying to protect me. But I'm twenty-five. I need to follow my path. She had her chance to follow hers."

"I get it. I was lucky since there were three of

us it wasn't as hard. Have you explained it to her like that?"

"No, not yet. But that's a good idea." Meghan smiled and popped the trunk of the car. Stowing Miranda's bag, they got into the car and headed to her apartment.

"I didn't want to tell you right away, but I have some bad news," Meghan started, but Miranda cut her off. Hearing the words 'bad news' twisted her insides into a knot and the worst possible thoughts entered her mind.

"What news? Is Cam okay?"

"Easy, everyone is fine as far as I know. I didn't mean to freak you out. They're going to be delayed. Something came up and their schedule got changed."

"But they're okay?"

"Yup. Rafe couldn't tell me anything other than they weren't coming back yet and he'd let me know when they were on their way home."

"I wonder why Cam didn't let me know?"

"They were in a hurry, I told Rafe I'd let you know. I hope that's okay."

"Yeah, of course. But now you're stuck with me. I can get a hotel room until they get back."

"Don't be ridiculous. You can hang out and we can get to know each other better. Charlie talks about you all the time."

"He talks about you too. He's pretty chatty for a guy, isn't he?"

"Oh hell yeah. My sister, Lizzie, used to bitch at him all the time for telling all our secrets to anyone he met."

"That's funny."

"It is now, but it was absolute hell in high school. Oh my God, I remember when Lizzie had a huge crush on this guy on the Lacrosse team and Charlie told him. I thought she was going to kill him until Eric asked her to the prom. Then she didn't mind so much," Meghan said with a chuckle.

"I didn't have to worry about stuff like it. I used to wish for a sister to share secrets with. I think that's why I enjoy being part of the missionary group. Most of them have become my friends, some closer, like Charlie. It's like having sisters and brothers now."

"I guess I never thought of it that way. We always seem to want what we don't have, right?"

"Yeah, I guess that's true. How are you doing? I bet you miss Rafe."

"I do, but I've been keeping busy working on my book. I also went to Atlanta twice to check on my mom and help my sister. Did Charlie tell you our mom was diagnosed with Alzheimer's last year?"

"He did. I'm so sorry. It's a horrible disease."

"It is, but since we caught it early they are trying some of the newer drugs. Lizzie also found out about a new drug trial for some new 'miracle' drug. We're hoping we can get her in."

"That's great. If you have trouble maybe my dad can help try to get her in. Sometimes it helps to know people."

"That would be freaking great. Thank you so much. Do you think he'd help? I feel bad that most of mom's care falls on my sister since she's there. Plus she has her kids and a husband who travels constantly. I try to go and help out when I can."

"When I get back home, I'll be happy to help out. I love kids and old people," Miranda said with a smile. It was true, she enjoyed being around most people. There were just a few who'd been part of the missionary team on their last trip that had gotten on her last nerve. Not everyone who joined the group was religious, most of them, like her, had joined to help the girls in Afghanistan and it was the best way to do it.

"Thank you, that's so sweet of you. Maybe while you're here we can Skype with Lizzie and you can meet her and the kids. They are a piece of work."

"How old are they?"

"Ten going on twenty and they're twins. Lia and Craig."

"Twins? How cool is that?"

"Yeah, I said the same thing. So did Lizzie until her husband was away on business and she was alone with two newborns. Then it wasn't so cool."

"I hadn't thought about that. How come he travels so much?"

"His job, he's in software applications and trying to move up the 'food chain' hoping to get a VP job so he can be home more."

"That would be good. I'm sure Lizzie would be grateful."

"Shit, you have no idea. And we're here. That was one of the most pleasant rides from the airport ever. Hardly any traffic and no back-ups in the tunnel. You must be good luck."

"I doubt it, but I'm happy it worked today." The two women were still smiling when they went into the condo. The first thing Meghan did was show Miranda her room and then she turned on the news. Meghan had wanted to be a foreign correspondent but after what she went through in Afghanistan trying to save her brother, she'd decided to stick to blogs and was writing a book instead. From what Cam had told her, Meghan's blog was doing great and she was making decent money.

"Still addicted to the news?" Miranda asked as she joined Meghan in the living room.

"Yeah, I can't help it. Especially when the guys are deployed. It's like my little link to Rafe. We may not know where they are, but if there's trouble and they're deployed it's a pretty good guess they're in the middle of it."

"I do the same thing. At first, I would drive myself crazy trying to figure out where they'd been sent. But this deployment has been the worst."

"It hasn't been fun, that's for sure. But we won't have to wait much longer. They'll be home soon."

Miranda envied Meghan's calm composure. She felt like she was constantly on edge. Worried that something would happen to Cam before they could get to know each other.

"I hope so."

"Hey, it'll be okay. I have an idea. How about I invite Chrissy to come over and we can have a girl's night? Watch chick flicks, eat pizza, and drink way too much wine."

"That sounds great."

"I'll give her a call. The menu for the pizza place is in the drawer next to the stove, can you grab it so we can order."

~

THE TRANSPORT TOUCHED DOWN IN RIYADH,

Saudi Arabia, just after dawn. They'd landed on one of the regular runways and taxied to the back of the General Aviation Terminal. Air Force One would be landing at the Royal Terminal in three and a half hours. The clock was ticking.

"Remember, we're not here, so stay under the radar as well as you can," Captain Knox said as they grabbed their gear. It wasn't necessary to remind them how to do their jobs, but with the importance of the mission, Cam understood why he did it. Not that they all weren't important, but this was POTUS.

"We'll take out the tangos, diffuse the threat and be back before you know it," Jake responded for all of them.

"You might need to leave Halo here, Cam," Knox said as they grabbed their gear.

"He'll be fine, Captain. Besides, he'll sniff out the explosive materials before any of us could find them."

"I think we need him, Captain. As a safeguard. Halo knows how to stay low, don't you, boy?" Jake said, and Knox nodded. Halo acted like he understood the whole conversation. As soon as Knox said his name he sat down and looked forlorn, but once Jake spoke, he was back on his feet with his tail wagging.

Activating the camera on Halo's collar was the last thing Cam did as they exited the plane. The clock was down to three hours. Dressed like the locals, they did their best to blend in. They separated as they entered the airline terminal and arranged to meet up at the first rendezvous point.

Navigating through the airport with Halo took Cam longer than expected. The children wanted to pet him, and to maintain his cover he let them. A few asked about the camera on Halo's collar and he told them it was a charm. Finally, he met up with the team at the Taxi Stand in front of the airport.

Lynch's contact had arranged for a van to take them to a local coffee shop for the meetup. So far, so good. The vehicle was waiting as expected. It was almost too easy. Usually, there was at least one issue they'd have had to deal with. They didn't know Lynch's contact, and he hadn't figured out who the mole was yet, so they could be walking into a trap. Time would tell. Jake's voice came through his earpiece, "radio silence until we know this isn't a setup."

"Copy that," the team replied. Cam's gut screamed at him that something wasn't right, but nothing looked out of place as the van navigated the streets of Riyadh. Ten minutes later they stopped in front of the Camel Step Coffee Roasters on Abi Bakr As Siddiq Road.

"Watch your six," Jake murmured, and they nodded. The streets were packed with people and the coffee shop was no exception. Grabbing a table outside since they had Halo, Jake sent Murph in with the driver to get the coffee.

A few minutes later, they returned. Lynch and another man was with them. How he'd gotten there so quickly none of them knew, but it so far everything was on target. Splitting up so they didn't draw attention to themselves, they sat on opposite sides of the coffee shop doorway. With their coms, they'd hear everything.

"This is Naif, he's been my contact here for about five years. You can trust him," Lynch advised as they sat down with the coffee. Jake shook the man's hand, then they sat down.

"Naif, tell them what you told me," Lynch said, then took a sip of coffee and looked around. Halo sat at Cam's side, his ears twitching as he stayed alert. Cam bent down to rub his ears and reported two men he'd seen across the street taking photos.

If he hadn't been watching, Cam wouldn't have noticed the almost imperceptible nods from Jake and the team. Murph picked up another two on the other side of the street. That meant there were at least four men surveilling them, but how had they known they were going to be at the coffee shop. There wasn't a member of their team who believed in coincidences.

"Just a minute. Lynch, you said this guy was trustworthy."

"Yeah, why?"

"Then why are there four tangos tracking us?"

"What the fuck? Are you sure? Naif? What the fuck is going on?"

"Nothing. I made some inquiries as you asked. That is all. I did not mention the Americans. Or about your president."

"Who did you talk to?" Jake wasn't as laid back as Lynch. They didn't have time for this shit, they only had two hours and twelve minutes left.

"It was after morning prayers. I asked a few of the men in my Mosque. Then I sent my driver to the airport to pick up your men."

"We need the names of everyone you spoke to at the Mosque. Write them down and give them to Lynch. Rafe, you and Murph go take out our company. Then meet us at the van."

"Copy that, Boss."

Cam kept watch as Rafe and Murph took out the tangos one at a time.

"Now, Naif, I want to know everything you learned and don't leave out any details. If we find out you turned, you'll never see daylight again," Lynch said. If his asset had gone bad he could say goodbye to his career, especially if they lost POTUS.

After Naif told them everything, Jake questioned him on some of the details. Making sure nothing changed when he asked him several times. Then they left him and Lynch to do whatever and went back to the van. They needed to get out of there. It wouldn't be long until the dead men were discovered, and they wanted to be long gone.

Naif got behind the wheel with the instructions to drive them back to the airport. It was obvious that Jake didn't trust him and wanted to make sure he didn't know any more about their plan than necessary.

"What's the plan, Boss," Cam asked. They were huddled in the back of the van. Unless they were bugged, no one could hear what they discussed.

"We're going to split up. I don't like it but we're running out of time. Rafe, you take Murph and Ryan and check out the Mosque. Naif mentioned a guest house that's had a lot of activity lately. I think our buddy Azfaar might be holed up there."

"Copy that."

"Cam and I will search the Royal Terminal for any sign of explosives. I'll report back to TOC. Set your watches, rendezvous behind the terminal in forty-five mikes." When the van stopped at the next traffic light, they opened the door and blended in with the crowd.

By the time they got back to the airport, they'd

burned another twenty minutes due to traffic. He and Jake walked through the main terminal doors and split up. They'd meet up at the rear of the Royal Terminal and start searching for the bombs.

As he and Halo moved through the airport, he watched for any sign they were being followed. They made it all the way to the entrance of the Royal terminal wing before picking up a tail. Cam wasn't sure if it was the Royal Secret Service or the new ISIS Al-Qaeda team trying to take him out. Ducking out of sight, he picked the lock on a door marked "employees only," Cam and Halo slipped inside, and it was sheer luck that it was filled with janitorial uniforms and carts.

Changing into one of the uniforms, he tipped the cart for Halo to jump inside the garbage can and grabbed a second uniform for Jake. Not the best plan but it should give them access without standing out.

"Eagle 1, this is Eagle 5. I got us a couple of janitor uniforms."

"Copy that. Location?"

Cam told Jake where to find him and within minutes he was at the door. After he changed, they exited out the back of the room and into the terminal each with their own cleaning cart. Jake took the west side and check the adjacent area. Cam took the east side of the terminal where Air

Force One was supposed to land. As soon as they were clear, he let Halo out of his hiding place.

The rest of the team hadn't reported in and Cam wondered what they'd walked into. It was never good when they split up the team. They each had their strengths and were better together. Jake must have been thinking the same thing because moments later Jake's voice came over the com.

"Eagle 2, this is Eagle 1. Give me a sitrep."

At first, there was no answer. Cam kept searching but listened intently hoping to hear a response. Finally, Rafe responded.

"Eagle 1, this is Eagle 2. Birds have flown the coop, burned the plans. Looks like their mission is a go."

"Eagle 2 copy that. Return to the airport. Rendezvous with Eagle 5. We need to find that device."

"Eagle 1, from what we found here it looks like there's more than one."

"Eagle 2, copy that."

Fuck. So much for eliminating the threat before it got to the airport. It was probably already there. But so far they hadn't found anything. The clock was down to one hour and seventeen minutes. They needed to find the devices before the plane landed.

CHAPTER 3

CHRISSY AND THE PIZZA DELIVERY GUY SHOWED up at the same time. Even better, she came bearing ice cream and three bottles of Moscato. Miranda wondered if any of them would be able to stand up by ten p.m. It was her first girl's night ever, so she hadn't known what to expect.

While they were waiting for Chrissy and the pizza, she and Meghan picked out a bunch of movies, some Miranda hadn't seen. They had a mix of chick flicks and action movies with hunky men. It was a tossup about which would be better.

"I think we should start with the hunks. Let's save the girly movies for ice cream," Chrissy voted when Meghan asked for a preference.

"Sounds good to me. Which one should we go with?"

"How about Thor?"

"Hell yeah, and Loki isn't hard on the eyes either," Chrissy said and laughed. Miranda liked her already. Who knew that an FBI analyst could be so much fun?

While Meghan started the movie, she grabbed a slice of pizza and settled into the corner of the couch. Chrissy poured the wine and handed Miranda a glass. They gabbed more than watched the movie, commenting on abs and six packs. Loki was cute, in an evil sort of way, but damn that Chris Hemsworth was one sexy man and reminded her of Cam. She 'd tried not to think about where he was or worry about what he was doing. As much fun as she was having with Chrissy and Meghan, she'd been looking forward to seeing him.

"Hey, no moping. This is girl's night. We drink, eat too much, and laugh our asses off until we can't breathe. Those are the rules," Meghan said, and Chrissy nodded as she took another bite of pizza.

Determined to have a good time, she smiled, took a huge swallow of wine and asked, "How long have you known each other?"

"Me and Chrissy? Hell, we grew up together. So it's what? Almost thirty years?"

"At least," Chrissy agreed.

"Thirty? I didn't realize you were that much older than Charlie."

"He's the baby of the family and Lizzie is the oldest. I'm the problem child in the middle. Or at least that's what Mom used to say. I'll be thirty-two this year."

"I didn't mean you were old."

"I didn't take it that way." Meghan smiled and refilled her wine glass. "Now drink up. We have two more bottles to finish."

"We're going to drink all that wine? Three bottles?"

"The only rules are to have fun, remember? That's all that matters."

"Miranda, haven't you done this with your friends?" Chrissy asked.

"Not really. We'd go to the movies, out to dinner, but never anything like this. I guess it was partly my parents, they were always strict about who I could be friends with and what I did. They called it being careful, I called it being overprotective and stifling. Then when dad became a senator there was security all the time. It was easier to just stay home until I joined the missionary group."

"Holy shit. Seriously? That doesn't sound like much fun," Meghan said.

"It was okay. I didn't think about it. It was just my life."

"You're not against drinking, are you? I know Charlie doesn't but it's not because of his faith, he just doesn't like it much. But I didn't even think you might not want to drink."

"Oh no, it's nothing like that. I'm not religious like that. I joined the missionary group to help build schools for the girls. I wanted to give back and it was a good option. Actually, it was how I got my father to agree. Although he didn't expect me to go overseas. That didn't go over well."

"I bet it didn't. I'd have loved to see the look on their faces when you told them," Meghan said.

"Yeah, it wasn't pretty. But I needed to do it for me. I want my own life. But after the abduction, it got worse. My mother practically loses it whenever I'm out of her sight. I told you how she wanted me to stay home and just have him visit."

"Fuck, that wouldn't have been much fun with her watching your every move."

"I'm too old for that. I have to make them understand it's time for me to live my life."

"Good for you. They're going to freak out when they find out you're going back, aren't they?" Meghan mused as she refilled their glasses.

Miranda didn't want to think about it. "I think we've talked enough about me. Let's drink to sexy movie stars, wine, and lots of calories."

Meghan and Chrissy raised their glasses, and Miranda drained hers in one huge gulp and hiccupped. "Oh, shit. Excuse me."

"Holy fuck, I'm rubbing off on you. You said

shit," Meghan said and started giggling. "Your parents are going to kill me."

"I've said it before. I'll say it again. Shit, shit, shit, damn, shit and hell." That set them all off and soon the movie was forgotten. Chrissy and Meghan told stories of all the trouble they'd gotten into in high school and college.

By the time Meghan brought out the ice cream, Miranda was stuffed on pizza and tipsy from all the wine.

"If I eat that I'll definitely lose it. I'm so full."

"Okay, I'll put yours back in the freezer, but I swear it's the perfect dessert after all of this."

"She's right you know. You think you can't, but you can."

"I'll pass for now. I'd rather have another glass of wine."

"Woohoo, look at you," Chrissy said as she passed the last bottle of wine to Miranda.

"Holy crap, we finished the other two already?"

"Yup. I told you," Meghan said with a giggle. "It's girl's night. Oh and what happens here, stays here. We don't share with the men."

"Gotcha. No sharing with the men," Miranda said as she held up three fingers in the scout's honor salute, which made them all laugh again. She couldn't remember the last time she'd laughed so much, and her ribs were hurting a bit. It was taking them forever to fully heal, but she'd handle the pain for this much fun anytime.

"I don't have to worry about that. No man for me," Chrissy said and pushed out her bottom lip in an exaggerated pout.

"Why not? You're beautiful, smart, funny," Miranda asked.

"That's the problem, I'm too smart. It intimidates most of the men I've dated," Chrissy said.

"That's because you date a bunch of fucktards. You need to go out with Ryan, I know he's interested," Meghan responded.

"Ryan? The SEAL medic?" Miranda asked.

"Yes. When he and Chrissy are both here, he can't take his eyes off of her."

"He was very gentle with me and I agree, he's really handsome. Not as gorgeous as Cam but still."

"I don't think it's a good idea."

"Why not?" Miranda and Meghan asked in unison.

"Because if it doesn't work out it will be weird when we try to hang out. I don't want to not hang out with you and he and Rafe are so close."

"That's bullshit. Besides, you don't know it won't work out."

"No, but with my track record, it's pretty likely. Besides he's a fuckin' SEAL. He can screw any woman in Norfolk. Why pick someone that's in his inner circle?"

"But you never know," Miranda asked. It didn't make sense to not try. Life was short and full of surprises. "I think you like him. You should take a chance. After what I just went through, it taught me that tomorrow isn't guaranteed and if you want something you need to go for it."

Chrissy seemed to consider what she said and nodded. "That's true. But to tell you the truth, I like my life the way it is. I don't have to worry about anyone else, it doesn't matter if I work long hours or weekends, no one is there but the cat to care."

"And you think Ryan wouldn't understand about that? Hell, they're gone at a moment's notice."

"I think you're just making excuses. If you want to be single, that's cool, but if you like him then I say go for it. I know I don't know you well yet, but you said we can say whatever we want tonight."

"That's true. You caught on quick."

"I might be sheltered but I'm not stupid."

"We never thought you were."

"I think I'll have that ice cream now."

"You got it," Meghan went to grab it from the freezer. Chrissy turned to her when they were alone. "How are you doing for real? I know you said you were okay, but you went through a lot."

"I did, but I'm okay. Having Charlie to talk to helps. I still have nightmares but they're happening less often."

"Good. Meghan has them. Rafe told me, she's stubborn too. You are a lot alike."

"Stop talking about me, I can hear you."

"What? We're not saying a thing."

"Yeah. Yeah. So Rafe told you I was having nightmares?"

"Maybe."

"Well, I didn't tell you."

"He wanted me to make sure you were okay while he was gone. That's all."

"He's a good man," Meghan said with a huge smile.

"Yes, he is."

"So is Cam," Meghan added.

"I know. It doesn't seem real sometimes. Life is strange."

"I'll drink to that," Chrissy said, and they finished the last of the Moscato and dug into their ice cream. Miranda definitely needed more female companionship. It was time for her to make some changes.

THE CLOCK WAS TICKING, WITH LESS THAN AN hour left, they still hadn't found any trace of the explosives.

"Eagle 5, this is Eagle 1, sitrep."

"Eagle 1, negative for the explosives. Halo hasn't picked up anything."

"Copy that Eagle 5. I'm negative here too."

"Eagle 1, this is Eagle 2, we're at the terminal."

"Copy that Eagle 2. Come through the maintenance door and rendezvous with Eagle 5."

"Copy that, Eagle 1."

"C'mon boy," Cam called Halo as he headed toward the rear of the terminal. He was starting to wonder if the intel had been wrong and there weren't any explosives.

Rendezvousing in the cover of the luggage carts, they discussed their next move.

"I don't get it. If there were explosives we'd have found them by now."

"Maybe we're looking in the wrong place," Rafe said. "The guest house had bomb-making material spread out across two tables. Someone was making explosive devices."

"But no sign of Azfaar?"

"Nope," Murph responded. "But he might have been warned by the guys we took out at the coffee shop."

"We're running out of time and JSOC is

giving the captain a rash of shit. We need to either verify the all clear or find the threat."

"What if they aren't out here yet?" Cam asked.

"What are you thinking?" Jake responded.

"If they were tipped off that we're here, they wouldn't have them planted where we could find them."

"Plausible. So what, suicide vests?"

"Maybe, or maybe they'll use something to approach the plane after it's landed."

"Good point. We haven't found any trace out here or around the terminal. If the intel is good, then the tangos are most likely inside the terminal waiting to be activated," Jake said.

"Cam, you and Halo continue to search the perimeter. Halo would be the first to detect explosives. Ryan and Murph take the right side of the terminal, Rafe you're with me. If we find any tangos, we need to take them out quietly. We're not here."

"Copy that." Ryan and Murph slipped back inside the terminal. Jake called the captain to give him a sitrep and advise him of the updated plan.

"And you were bored," Rafe said and grinned at Cam.

"Yeah, well. That'll teach me to bitch out loud."

"Fucking yeah. But it's not every day we get to save the leader of the free world."

"If we can find the threat in time."

"We will and no one will know but us."

"Exactly," Jake said as he came up behind Rafe. "Let's go. Cam, you good?"

"Of course."

"Advise asap of any persona non grata."

"Copy that. Notify asap of PNG activity," Cam confirmed as he and Halo slipped into the shadows to check the perimeter. Staying hidden, they rechecked every nook and cranny they could find that would be large enough to plant an explosive. It wouldn't take much to ignite the plane. Just one spark near the fuel tank and it would go up like a roman candle on the Fourth of July.

It was frustrating, knowing that the threat existed but being unable to find it. It's not how they operated. Find the threat, eliminate it, and move on to the next one. The lack of any sign of explosives made Cam wonder if it had been a false trail to take them off the scent of the real threat. Maybe it would be a bomb directed toward the presidential motorcade.

That's when he saw it. The fueling tanker. It approached what looked like one of the Saudi prince's planes on the other side of the terminal. It made perfect sense. It wouldn't take more than a small ignition to turn the tanker into a bomb.

"Eagle 1, this is Eagle 5."

"Go ahead Eagle 5."

"I think they're going to use the refueling tanker," Cam said into his com. Even though he directed his message to Jake the entire team would hear it.

"Copy that, Eagle 5. Everyone rendezvouses at the checkpoint."

The clock kept ticking. Air Force One was due in fifteen minutes. They needed to secure the area and remove all threats or wave off the plane, and they were running out of time.

CHAPTER 4

EAGLE 1, THIS IS TOC." JAKE LOOKED AT THE team, before responding to Captain Knox. They didn't have confirmation that the terrorists would use the fuel tanker as the bomb, but it made the most sense.

"Eagle 1, go ahead TOC."

"I need a sitrep. Has the threat been contained?"

"No, it hasn't. But we think we figured it out."

"I'm supposed to tell the general that POTUS is safe to land because you *think* you figured it out?" As Cam listened to the exchange he winced at the captain's words.

"Yes, sir. I do," Jake responded.

"If anything happens to that plane our careers are over. You do realize that, Master Chief?"

"Yes, sir. I believe we can neutralize the threat in time."

The silence was worse than an ass chewing, and it was taking too long for a response. Eating into their window. Halo stood up and let out a low growl, but loud enough for Cam to hear. As he turned toward the direction of Halo's line of sight, he saw two tangos running along the edge of the terminal. If the dog hadn't picked up on their scent, he'd never have known they were there.

Before he could alert the team, their coms echoed with the captain's response. "POTUS is on final approach, but we can still wave him off. You'd better be right, Eagle 1. You have five mikes."

"Copy that. Eagle 1 out."

"We've got two tangos at nine o'clock," Cam said.

"This is what we've been waiting for. Follow but don't engage until we're sure they are the threat."

"Copy that."

Cam and Halo took point. Ryan and Murph swung around to try to head them off, while Rafe and Jake followed closely behind. As they followed the tangos, they ran for a fuel tanker that had been parked beyond the terminal at the edge of one of the runways.

"Eagle 1, tangos are hot and heading for the truck."

"Eagle 3, do you have eyes on the target?"

"Copy that, Eagle 1," Ryan responded. "Eagle 4 has a clear shot."

"Take them out before they reach that tanker."

"Copy that, Eagle 1."

As Cam watched, first one then the other tango went down. They dropped before he heard the sound of the rifle. "Eagle 5, secure the tanker."

"Copy that, Eagle 1." Cam and Halo ran for the tanker, as Ryan and Murph checked the tangos. Murph was their sniper and Cam was impressed every time he saw him work. It didn't matter how difficult the shot, he'd made it.

They reached the tanker and Halo checked it for explosives. There was a detonator attached near the fuel hose, but it wasn't armed.

"Eagle 1, tanker is secure. Threat is eliminated."

"Copy that, Eagle 5," Jake responded. "Eagle 1 to TOC. The threat is neutralized, I repeat threat is neutralized."

"Never doubted you, Eagle 1," Captain Knox replied, but the relief was plain to hear in his voice. "Head to the EXFIL so we can get the fuck out of here."

"Copy that, TOC."

"I don't think we could have cut that closer if we tried," Murph said as they headed to their plane. They'd accomplished the mission without alerting the locals or tipping off the Secret Service. Just another day at the office, except there was no going home and discussing their day with the families.

After they were airborne, Cam breathed a sigh of relief. For him, the mission never felt completed until they were in the air. He wasn't sure why, but it had been that way since the beginning.

"We're cleared for home. Red Falcon Team has landed at Bagram."

"I say that calls for a celebration. Who wants a beer?" Jake asked as he headed over to the cooler. They kept a stash on board for after missions, and if any of them deserved to be celebrated it was this one. POTUS wouldn't know he'd been in danger until the Joint Chiefs briefed him. It was a win or at least part of one, they hadn't caught the fucktards behind the plot. Azfaar was still out there and it was guaranteed that he'd be causing more trouble.

Cam grabbed a beer, then set out food and water for Halo, before he sat down. He wanted to call Miranda and let her know they were on the way.\ While he was figuring out the time difference, Rafe sat next to him.

"You know you can't tell her about the mission."

"Seriously? You're fucking reminding me like I'm some kind of newbie? That I don't know all of our missions are top secret?"

"I'm just saying. They don't all involve your girlfriend's father. The temptation will be there."

Cam hadn't thought about it. He'd never been tempted to share information about their missions with anyone, but then this was the first time he was in a real relationship. He'd dated plenty, but nothing was ever serious until Miranda, she was different.

"How do you handle it with Meghan?"

"She knows that I can't talk about it and doesn't ask. It was a little different on the deployment because we were mostly training."

"We haven't been on any missions until now since you've gotten together. either."

"True."

"Just because I'm younger than you, Grandpa, doesn't mean I need to be reminded," Cam replied as he hid his irritation with sarcasm. It was true, he was a SEAL and knew the rules just as much as the rest of them.

"You're right, kid," Rafe said with a wink. "I just know how anxious you've been to get home to her."

"No more so than you are."

"Touché."

"What are you two whispering about," Murph asked as he sauntered toward them with refills. Relieved that the focus was off of him, Cam grabbed one of the bottles.

"Nothing. Just talking about living arrangements," Cam said and gave Rafe a look that dared him to disagree with what he'd said.

"Miranda's staying with Meghan since we were late. You never know what those women are up to."

"No shit. Women are worse than we are. They're probably talking about how often there will be a banana in the fruit salad."

"Fuck Murph, how do you come up with that shit?" Ryan asked.

"Just how my mind works, bro. Can't help it."

"You're just jealous," Cam added.

"Me? Hell to the fuck no. I like buttering the biscuit as much as anyone, but I prefer a fresh one. Nothing stale for me."

"How's that?"

"It's the thrill of the hunt, like a crap shoot. Sometimes you miss, sometimes you hit, but you never know until you try."

"And the women you're with don't care?"

"Not so far. I think most of the women at The Ready Room expect it."

"You're nothing but a horndog," Jake said as

he joined the group. "One of these days one of those women is going to catch you like a bass on a hook."

"That's what you think. This frogman will never be hooked."

"That's a bet I'll take," Cam said with a huge grin. Now that Rafe was with Meghan it was like something had changed with everyone else. He saw it in Jake's eyes when he watched Rafe and Meghan together. It was Longing for what he didn't have.

"What are you talking about, kid?"

"A bet that you'll get caught by a woman. The only question is how long until it happens. But it will happen."

Murph laughed. "Fine, go ahead bet against me, but you're throwing your money away."

Jake laughed too. "Okay, so how are we going to do this? And who will hold the money?"

"I will," Bill Lynch said. "But I want in too. I've got fifty on Murph. No woman is gonna convince him to settle down. I've seen his moves in The Ready Room." Murph thumped him on the back.

"See, Lynch knows."

"You got it," Cam said as he wrote his bet down. "Next?"

"Wait, you're all putting money in, but what's the time frame. You can't leave it open-ended."

"Leave it to Ryan to pour ice on the deal."

"What the fuck, don't make me punch you. I'm just saying. We need to figure this shit out or it'll be a clusterfuck like our last bet. Remember, Jake?"

"Fuck yeah. Good point. Okay, so if Murph is still single in two years he wins, but if he's been 'hooked' then he loses."

Cam looked around and when none of the team objected, he wrote the 'rules' on the top of the betting list. "What happens when he loses?"

"There's no way I'm losing," Murph boasted then chugged his beer.

"We'll see about that. How about this," Jake continued, "if Murph loses he has to serve us beer in The Ready Room in a pink dress."

They howled loud enough that the captain wandered over. "I thought you would be sleeping by now. What's going on?"

"Just a friendly bet, Cap."

"Yeah, we're betting that Murph won't be single two years from now," Ryan explained.

"I want in," Tony Knox said as he pulled a few bills out of his wallet. "You won't make it, Murph. Sorry, bro. But as these guys find their women it's inevitable. Trust me."

"Gee, Cap, I thought for sure you'd take my side."

"Sorry. Been there done that."

Ryan, Rafe, and Jake put in fifty each against Murph, and Cam added his name to the list. After he double checked that he'd marked down all the bets, he added his money and totaled it up. Then he wrapped the two-hundred and fifty dollars inside the sheet listing the bets and handed it to Lynch.

"So, same deal as last time?" Cam asked.

"You mean with the money?" Jake nodded. "You all okay with that?"

"Yeah, money goes to the next fundraiser The Ready Room runs."

"With any luck, Murph will be wearing pink to the event."

"You've had too much beer, kid, because there ain't no way I'm losing this one."

Cam laughed. "We'll see." Grabbing some shut-eye sounded like a plan now that he'd had a couple of beers and the adrenaline from the missions had subsided. They had their spots in the plane and settled in for a well-deserved rest. Cam stretched out next to Halo. After figuring out the time zones, he didn't want to wake Miranda with a phone call, so he sent a text before he went to sleep.

~

MIRANDA FIGURED THAT THEIR GIRL'S NIGHT

was a success. They'd finished all three bottles of wine, the ice cream, and more than half the pizza. But most of all they'd laughed their butts off. She couldn't remember having such honest and funny conversations in her life. Chrissy and Meghan were unbelievable and the stories they'd told about their high school antics were amazing. She was shocked that they'd managed to graduate at all.

For Miranda, it had been a private school and all about the grades. Not that her childhood was horrible, her parents loved her, but they expected her to act like the good little senator's daughter and not get into any trouble. And she hadn't, until the kidnapping in Afghanistan. Go big or go home. They weren't going to be happy when they found out she was going back to the Middle East.

"Want to watch another movie?" Meghan asked. She must have nodded off at some point because the final credits for Moonstruck were playing. That was embarrassing, but luckily they didn't seem to notice.

"Sure," Chrissy said. "How about Die Hard, it's getting late and I could use some action and hell Bruce Willis ain't too shabby."

"No, kidding. That okay with you, Miranda?"

It was after two a.m. Miranda had been struggling and obviously had failed to stay awake for the last hour. It was time she went to bed or risk falling asleep on the couch. She couldn't do that. It would be rude since Chrissy and Meghan were still chattering away.

"Another movie? You two must do this a lot? I can't keep my eyes open and you're still going strong."

"We used to. Not so much lately. Now that I'm living with Rafe we make the most of them when we have them."

"That makes sense. I'll have to work on my staying power."

"No worries, Miranda," Chrissy said with a smile. "Hey, does anyone call you Randy?"

That stopped her as she'd started to get up. "Randy? Nope, definitely not. I can't even imagine my mother saying it."

"Ahh okay, I was just wondering."

"No problem, night."

"Night."

Randy? Not sure how she felt about that nickname or any nickname. She'd never had one, never even thought to shorten her name even though Miranda always seemed kind of old-fashioned. As she climbed in between the sheets and settled down, different names ran through her mind as she fell asleep.

It was still dark when she woke up drenched in sweat and crying. The clock said four-thirty, so she hadn't been asleep for long. After listening to make sure she hadn't woken the other women, she got up and went to the bathroom.

It was the same nightmare each time. Dark figures would break into their tent and drag her away from the others. Then they'd cover her face with a foul-smelling hood. She pleaded with them to let her go, but they laughed and spoke Pashto so quickly she couldn't figure out what they were saying. Only one part of the dream had changed over the months since her rescue—now she screamed for Cam to save her. And it was his face she focused on to survive the torture.

A cold shower helped clear her mind. Sliding into one of Cam's old Navy t-shirts, she sat in the chair by the window in her room. Peeking out through the blinds at the star-filled night, she wondered if he was thinking of her. His three-month deployment had seemed like an eternity but now that she'd see him soon, she was worried.

They hadn't been together in months, and before that, it was just a few days at a time. The connection had been so intense when he'd found her in the cave, and they'd saved her and the other missionaries. Her father insisted she was just grateful, and that Cam was using her to get help up in his career. But he didn't know Cam as she did, and that was the thing. Did she know him?

She used to love the stillness of the night, the quiet, but now she was restless, even when she didn't have the nightmares. It was time for some major soul-searching to decide what she wanted. She had already agreed to go on the next trip to help with the school, but then she'd see about moving to Virginia if things worked out with Cam. Surely, she could find another way to help without traveling back to the land of her nightmares.

CHAPTER 5

THE SUN PEEKED THROUGH THE OPEN BLINDS when Miranda opened her eyes for the second time. Relief that she'd managed to sleep for a few hours without another nightmare, brought a smile to her face. Double nightmares didn't happen often but when they did it was horrible, and most of the time it was after she'd been stressed. The wine and worrying about Cam being stuck in Afghanistan had most likely triggered this one.

Tip-toeing to the bathroom to take a shower and get ready for the day, she heard the women in the kitchen. Wondering if they'd slept at all, she jumped into the shower. As far as she knew, they didn't have any plans for today and dressed in jeans and a short-sleeved silk shirt. Maybe she could convince Meghan to take her shopping. It was time to buy clothes she liked instead of what her mother expected her to wear.

"Good morning."

Meghan turned and greeted her with a big smile. "Good morning, Sunshine. How are you?"

The question told Miranda that her nightmare hadn't gone unnoticed and she hoped she hadn't disturbed them. "I'm fine. Did you sleep at all?"

Chrissy laughed. It was the infectious type. You couldn't listen to her and not at least smile. "Sure. Maybe an hour. Tomorrow is going to be totally suckful. Thank God it's the weekend."

"No shit. But there is the nectar of the gods at our disposal and we shall imbibe copious amounts until we resemble humans."

"What the hell are you talking about? You used way too many big words for this little sleep." If Miranda hadn't been looking right at her, she'd have thought she was serious, but obviously, this was another conversation they'd had often.

"I could use copious amounts of that nectar."

"I bet. How do you take it?"

"I'm a wimp. Three sugars and some of that half-and-half."

"Three? You like it sweet. No wonder you like Cam. He's such a sweetie too," Chrissy replied as she handed Miranda the mug of coffee.

"He is, isn't he? Strange to say that about a

Navy SEAL. The ones I'd met with my father always seemed so serious."

"They were on official duty then, not just hanging out. They are all sweet, well most of them anyway. I've met a few that were real jerks."

"That's guys for you, some are just asshats."

"No shit. But you were lucky with Rafe, me too because it got you to move here."

"Yup. So that makes me doubly lucky."

"I'm thinking about moving here too. If I can find a job after I get back from the next trip to Afghanistan."

"Really?" Meghan hugged her, and almost spilled her coffee. "What triggered that? Oh, I bet it was girl's night."

"I won't lie. Girl's night was a definite draw. I want to help women who can't help themselves, but I honestly don't want to go back to Afghanistan. I feel like a wimp even saying it out loud."

"No, you are not even close to a wimp. After everything you went through, how can you think that? No fucking way. I doubt most people would go back."

"It wasn't just me who was taken, the others in the missionary group are going back. I will too, I promised. But this will be the last time, and I'm scared shitless."

Meghan sat her down at the kitchen table and

then refilled her coffee mug. "Listen to me. I heard you last night, and no you're not the only one with nightmares. I don't like to admit it but it's nothing to be ashamed about. You went through hell and came out the other side. Do you know how amazing that is?"

"I didn't do anything. I just sat there until Cam and the team saved me."

"No, you survived. You. Survived. That was fucking hard, I know just how hard."

Chrissy sat across from Miranda and nodded her head with a solemn expression on her face. "It's true. I've been through this with Meghan too. Have you been to counseling?"

"No. I guess I didn't want to have to explain it to anyone else."

"Damn, you and Meghan could be twins. But luckily Rafe made her go. Tell her, Meggy. You know it helped."

"Yes, I have to admit, it did help. If you want, I'll call Dr. Marsh and see if she can fit you in while you're here. She's wonderful."

"Maybe. I'll think about it. I promise. If they guys don't get back soon, then maybe."

"Didn't you check your phone yet? They're on their way. Should be here in a few hours if my math is right."

"Really?" Miranda couldn't contain her excitement and trepidation. Their relationship was still so new, and she'd been making lots of decisions about her future, some of them based on a relationship with him. What if he didn't want a long term relationship with her?

"Whatever you're thinking, just stop," Meghan said. "I hope you don't play poker because everything you think shows up plain as day on your face."

"Yeah, I know. I could never fool my parents."

"What are you worried about?" Chrissy asked.

"Me. Cam. Us. I don't know. We've had a half dozen dates, lots of phone calls and Skype calls, but I'm not the same girl he rescued or the one who was recovering the last time we were together. What if he doesn't like this version of me?"

"Why wouldn't he? You're amazing?"

"No, I'm not. I'm just me, trying to find a way to help in this world."

"And you can't see yourself the way others do. You're sweet, caring, and innocent of so much."

"I'm not innocent. I may have been sheltered growing up..." Miranda ruffled at the words she'd heard most of her adult life.

"Maybe that was a poor choice, but you still believe in so much good. You're not jaded by the reality of life like so many others. You're a bright light in the darkness. I'm sure that's what Cam sees."

"Really? Because I don't feel that way at all."

Meghan hugged her again and looked into her eyes. "Don't worry about Cam. He's one of the good guys. If Halo loves him he has to be."

"That's true. Dogs are the best judge of character ever," Chrissy said. "Maybe I need to get a dog."

"You could have Ryan." Miranda hadn't meant to say that out loud. But when she'd come to the housewarming party for Meghan and Rafe, she'd seen the way the big SEAL had watched every move Chrissy had made. His eyes followed her everywhere.

"Didn't we have this discussion last night? Were you two so drunk you don't remember?"

"I remember, but I also know how he looks at you."

Miranda nodded. "And when I was here for the one party, he watched you all night. He never took his eyes off of you."

"You're both crazy, or maybe just hungover and imagining this shit. He hasn't said more than two words to me since I met him at the party."

"Maybe he's shy." Miranda giggled as she said it. Shy? The big SEAL was the last person she'd call shy.

"He probably isn't sure if you're interested."

"What am I supposed to do? Hang up a shingle? Sexy SEALs apply here?"

"Oh my God, I can't believe you just said

that," Miranda snorted and almost spewed coffee across the table.

"See what I have to deal with? I hope you move here. We'll be like the three musketeers."

"That would be great. But first I have to get through the next trip and figure out what I can do for work."

"I'm sure you'll find something. You can always move in with me if you want," Chrissy offered.

"Thank you. That's so sweet of you. But I might be a horror to live with, you hardly know me."

"I think we fixed most of that last night, Sunshine."

"Where is this Sunshine coming from?"

"Oh, sorry. It's what Cam calls you when he talks about you."

"He calls me sunshine? And he talks about me?"

Meghan laughed. "Are you kidding? He doesn't stop talking about you when he visits. Not so much around all the guys but definitely around Rafe. I think he feels like it's something they have in common. Both having rescued their 'girls' from danger."

"I hadn't thought about that."

"Yeah. Everything is 'sunshine this and sunshine that' until Rafe threatens to drown him in the ocean if he says your name one more time. He's kidding of course. It's so funny."

"Wow. I had no idea. I was worried I was more a fling really. That if I was here all the time he'd feel pressured."

"I can't speak for him, but I bet if you tell him what you're thinking he'll be thrilled."

"I'm so surprised."

"I told you that you were amazing," Chrissy said as she poured another cup of coffee.

"You guys weren't kidding when you said you drank a lot of coffee," Miranda commented as she watched Chrissy set up another pot to brew.

"Nope. We're hardcore." Meghan giggled. "Maybe we should come up with a team name and get tattoos. We can be the Coffee Crew or something?"

"I'm up for it. I might have to be drunk first though."

"You're not allowed to be drunk when you get one."

"Says who?"

"The rules."

"And when have I followed them, or you for that matter. Hell, Beyotch, you went to Afghanistan to rescue your brother from the Taliban on your own. If that's not breaking the rules then I don't know what is."

Miranda had to agree with Chrissy's assessment, but she wasn't too thrilled with the idea of a tattoo. Maybe the idea would grow on her like a butterfly emerging from a cocoon. She was coming into her real self.

"I'm going to grab my phone to see if Cam sent me a text. When I get back I'm going to make us something to eat before we float away on the coffee express." Their laughter followed her down the hallway to her room.

There were several messages on her phone and not just from Cam. Her mother had called five times, texted three times, and sent email. She loved her, but dang it, she needed to start letting go. She'd always been over-protective but now it was crazy, and she felt stifled. It's the main reason she'd been trying to figure out what she wanted.

Choosing to read Cam's text messages first, she clicked on the first one.

Cam: We are almost back to the states. Can't wait to see you.

Reading his words helped ease the worry that had been causing her stomach to do flip-flops. Not that she hadn't believed Meghan, but she couldn't help herself. She'd never felt about anyone the way she did with Cam.

Cam: We landed. Have to get clear then heading to Meghan's.

Miranda: Can't wait to see you. 😊

Not expecting him to answer, she'd clicked on

the first of her mom's text messages. But then his message popped up.

Cam: It won't be long now.

Miranda: Yay.

Before she had a chance to do anything else, she heard the apartment door open and Meghan's squeal as she yelled Rafe's name. Her mother's messages ignored, she dropped the phone on the bed and ran out of the room.

CHAPTER 6

"REMEMBER, NOTHING ABOUT HER FATHER."

"Fuck you, Rafe. I'm a SEAL, not your little brother. I know not to say anything."

"Just a sanity check, okay."

"Got it. Now leave it alone. Or I'll have Halo take a bite out of your happy ass and we'll see how Meghan likes that."

Rafe laughed. Halo wouldn't bite him no matter what Cam said, but Rafe didn't know that for sure. He hid his smile as he watched Rafe glance in the rearview to check on Halo.

The last couple of miles dragged until his Sunshine answered his text messages. Rafe told him they'd had a girl's night and would most likely have drunk a lot. It explained why she hadn't answered his earlier texts right away.

Not being able to see her more often was hard,

and then the deployment complicated matters even further. Somehow she'd wormed her way into his heart. At first, it was all about keeping her calm, getting her out of that cave without hurting her further. But her toughness had impressed him. No whining as they'd expected, and she'd earned their respect.

The more time he spent with her the more he wanted to spend. She was like a breath of fresh air in his life. A special operator saw the worst in the world, and she was his sunshine. But would she want to deal with the life he led?

"Stop worrying, kid. If she didn't care, she wouldn't be at our place waiting for you."

"I know. It's just something her father said, that I'm playing out of my league."

"Fuck him. He has no idea."

"He might. He is ex-CIA."

"They're a bunch of pansy asses."

"Don't let Lynch hear you say that."

"No shit, right? It doesn't matter what her father thinks. She's a grown woman."

"A grown woman who still lives at home."

"But you said it wasn't her choice. Besides, she needed a place to recover. Right?"

"Take a breath. You're a SEAL. You've got this."

He'd better since Rafe pulled his truck into the

parking space and turned off the ignition. "Ready?"

"Hell yeah. Halo." Cam pulled the seat forward for the dog to get out. He looked just as excited to be home as they were.

As soon as Rafe's key turned in the lock, they heard Meghan's squeal. Then she flew into his arms when he opened the door.

"Get a room."

Meghan pulled back from kissing Rafe and gave him a smile. "Well hello to you too, froggy. Nice to see you and Halo."

Cam smiled and gave her a kiss on the cheek while she was still in Rafe's arms. "Thanks for taking care of Sunshine."

"We had a blast. Rafe, you'd better put me down before Cam knocks us over to get to his woman."

"It's my house if I want to stand in the doorway kissing my woman, then I will."

Cam laughed. He'd find a way to get him back for this, and payback was always a bitch.

When he finally pushed Rafe out of the way, he got his first look at the woman who'd filled his thoughts for the last three months. His Sunshine was standing in the kitchen doorway next to Chrissy. She was even more beautiful than the last time he'd seen her, and she took his breath away. Her wavy pale blonde hair looked like spun silk as it framed her face and his fingers itched to sift through the tresses.

Focused on his target, he strode across the living room and pulled Miranda into his arms. She was real, not a vision. Warm, soft, and finally his. "Hello, Sunshine."

"Hey." She sounded almost shy and a pang of worry sliced through his joy. He'd deal with it if she'd changed her mind about them, but he'd never get over her.

Still holding her in his arms, he leaned his head close to hers and whispered, "I've been waiting for this for ninety-one days, twelve hours, and sixteen minutes. Can I please kiss you?" He waited for what seemed like an eternity for her to answer him. But it was only a heartbeat or two.

Instead of words, she leaned closer until her lips touched his, and she slid her arms around his neck. All the tension drained as he kissed her with all the feelings that had been pent up for months. Pouring all his passion into that kiss and sliding his tongue inside and tasting her as she responded.

"Umm, get a room will ya?" Rafe said over Cam's shoulder. Reality came rushing back as he realized where he was. Setting Miranda onto her feet, her cheeks were bright pink and made her blue eyes shine even brighter. Her hair was tousled, and she looked well loved. All he could think about was getting her all alone and showing her how much he'd missed her. Mouthing the word "sorry," he turned around and almost tripped over Halo who had followed him and was now getting lots of loving from Miranda.

"I learned from the best," Cam responded to Rafe with a wink.

"I suppose you did. Just remember all the lessons." Cam bit his tongue instead of replying. The last thing he wanted was to discuss any of this in front of the women, not because they were women, but they were civilians. Rafe had deliberately baited him like he was testing him. He could see it if he was new to the team, but he'd been with them long enough to have proven himself. Maybe it was just part of the process. Since he'd never had a serious relationship before, and certainly not with anyone who related to their missions, maybe it was protocol. If it kept up, he'd go to Jake though, because it was already old.

"Are you okay? No injuries? I can't believe I'm here with you," Miranda said as she grasped his hand.

"I'm fine, we're all good. I can't believe it either. I'm so glad you're here though."

"Me too. And even though I missed you last night, hanging out with Meghan and Chrissy was so much fun. They're hysterical."

"Yes, and troublemakers."

"Who? Us?" Chrissy asked as she overheard their conversation. "We didn't do anything."

"Nope, they weren't troublemakers at all, except for loading me with calories."

"Well, that's no big deal. You'd be perfect no matter what." He hadn't meant to make her blush again.

"You nailed that one, Cam. Good for you," Chrissy said with a laugh.

"What's going on over there?" Meghan asked looking like she needed to recover from Rafe's greeting. As soon as Cam had pushed past him, he'd carried Meghan through the door and closed it behind them. He had quite the technique.

"Nothing at all. Just complimenting Cam on his silver tongue."

"Oh really?" Rafe laughed. "Now this I've got to hear."

'No, you don't." Miranda surprised them all when she answered.

Meghan elbowed Rafe in the side and laughed. "She sure told you." Cam laughed too, but when he saw Miranda's face he whispered into her ear, "it's okay. You are fine. And I love that you stuck up for me." His words relaxed her, and she grinned.

"You'll get used to all of us soon. We're just one big family," Cam said. "And now that you,

Meghan and Chrissy are part of it, it's a bit bigger."

Rafe nodded. "Exactly."

"I'm part of the family too?" Chrissy asked, obviously surprised to be included.

"Of course, silly. You're my best friend, you damn well better be included," Meghan said.

"But I'm not part of a couple…"

"That doesn't matter. Geesh, woman, do you think we're that shallow. We're SEALs, not jack-asses," Rafe said before Meghan could answer.

"He's right, you came with Meghan, kind of like a packaged deal," Cam added, and Miranda laughed.

"A package deal?"

"Yeah, that works. Doesn't it?"

"I guess kind of. But I might have chosen a different way to say it."

"I guess my silver-tongued status is lost, huh?"

"Nah, I wouldn't say that, maybe just a little tarnished. We'll have you shined up in no time," Chrissy said and giggled.

Cam rolled his eyes, that woman worried him. She was too smart and was always up to some-thing with Meghan.

"How long do you have off?" Miranda asked the question first. He'd been wondering if it would be her or Meghan.

"Since we're just back from deployment we

should get at least a week off. But as always it depends," Rafe answered and exchanged a look with Cam. Their status could change instantly and had more times than they could remember.

"Excellent. My return flight isn't until a week from Monday. I figured if it was too long and you had to go back to work, I could change it too."

"Perfect."

"Umm, this is going to sound weird but what are the living arrangements going to be for this trip? Miranda are you going to stay here with us…" Meghan's voice trailed off and left the sentence just hanging out there.

"She's staying with me, right Sunshine?" Cam answered before Miranda could, and hoped he'd said the right thing.

"Yeah, you two need your privacy after all this time. And if Cam pisses me off I'll go stay with Chrissy." His woman was getting feistier by the minute and it was one more thing to love about her.

"Sounds good. I'll be happy to have the company."

"I bet you would, but don't worry, she will be very happy with me."

"You know I'm standing here, right?"

Cam kissed her softly on the lips. "I'd never forget something like that."

"Now that's settled. How about some food. I

don't know about you, but Cam and I are starving."

Before he could agree with Rafe his stomach growled loud enough for all of them to hear.

"We have some leftover pizza, eggs, or we can go out."

"I vote for out. I don't think I can even look at another slice of pizza after last night," Chrissy said. Miranda nodded in agreement and Cam wondered if she'd tell him what this girl's night thing had entailed.

"How about the Ice House? They have just about everything," Rafe recommended. It was one of their favorites with excellent food and large servings. It was their first choice when they weren't going out to drink.

"That works for me. Miranda, is it okay with you?"

"Yup, it sounds good. I wasn't a fan of more pizza right now either."

"Maybe I should just head home. I feel like a fifth wheel."

"No way."

"How about I give Ryan a call? I'm sure he'd be up for joining us," Rafe said and pulled out his phone. Cam knew already that Ryan would be interested. He hadn't said much but it was obvious to the guys that he was interested in Chrissy. Rafe might know why he'd been holding back since they were close, but the rest of them didn't have a clue.

"Umm, you don't have to…"

"I know, but he's just as hungry as we are. If he doesn't want to come he won't."

The women exchanged a strange look and Cam would have to ask Miranda about it later. Chrissy was up to her usual something or other. He thought she might be interested in Ryan, but from the way she was acting, he could have been wrong.

Before anyone could say anything else, Ryan must have picked up the phone.

"Hey, bro, we're heading over to the Ice House. Want to come?" They could hear Rafe's side of the conversation, but Cam had a pretty good idea what Ryan was saying.

"No, just the women, me and Cam."

"Maybe fifteen minutes, give or take. You know how women are." That earned Rafe an elbow in the side hard enough to make him grunt and Cam chuckled. Meghan lived up to her spitfire nickname and then some. She was something else. As much as he thought she was amazing, he was glad that Miranda was softer and sweeter. He supposed that could change if she continued to hang out with the trouble twins.

"Perfect, see you there." Rafe disconnected the

call. "Okay, you heard me, we're out the door in fifteen so go do whatever you need to."

"Who says we need to do anything?" Meghan asked with her hands on her hips.

"Umm, no one. Just wanted to give you the option."

"Good thing or you might have found yourself sleeping in the recently vacated guest room."

Cam couldn't hold back his snort at the chagrin on Rafe's face. He'd barely extricated himself from that mess. And having learned from his friend's faux pas, he wasn't going to put his foot in his mouth.

"You look perfect already. Do you need to grab anything before we go?" He thought he was so suave until Rafe hit him in the back of the head.

"You trying to show me up, kid?"

"Maybe," Cam said with a huge grin. Not for getting back at Rafe but for the huge smile he'd earned from Miranda. It was like standing in the sunshine, and he'd never get enough of it.

"I wish you hadn't invited Ryan," Chrissy said, as she grabbed her purse.

"Why?" Cam and Rafe were surprised. Didn't she realize Ryan had a thing for her? Or maybe she didn't like him. He hadn't thought of that.

"He doesn't like me. He hardly says two words to me when he's here. It seems like you're just going to torture him with my presence. And trust me, as much as I like that idea, no one deserves that after a deployment."

"Don't worry, it won't be torture. He loves that food. If he comes up for air to acknowledge any of us I'll be freaking shocked," Rafe said.

"It'll be fine, stop being a fucking whiny-baby," Meghan said as she wrapped her arms around her friend. Oh yeah, there was definitely something going on.

They had to take two vehicles to the restaurant since Rafe's truck couldn't fit them all. Halo had to stay behind since the Ice House didn't allow non-service dogs. They'd tried before so he already knew it was a no-go. To take the sting out of staying behind, he opened a can of tuna and put it out for Halo along with some fresh water.

Then Cam and Miranda hitched a ride with Chrissy to make sure she didn't ditch them. By the time they arrived at the restaurant, Ryan was already leaning against the side of the building. If Cam hadn't been watching closely he wouldn't have seen Chrissy's intake of breath when she first saw him.

CHAPTER 7

THE FOOD AT THE ICE HOUSE WAS EXCELLENT, just as Cam said, but Miranda had trouble eating much. Nerves set in as she thought about being alone with him. She wasn't a prude or a virgin, but they hadn't had sex yet either. There had been plenty of kissing, touching, and intimacy but she hadn't been naked in front of him. When that thought hit her, her appetite had evaporated.

It's not that she had a poor self-image, she accepted her body for what it was—hers. She'd never felt the need to be perfect, or thin, or anything other than herself. But that had changed after Afghanistan. She'd been tortured. The men who took her had cut her so many times that most of her body was covered with scars. Since she'd been home, she'd made sure to be covered up most of the time.

"Don't you like the food?" Cam asked.

"Oh, it's wonderful, just like you said. I'm full already."

"But you hardly ate anything. Are you feeling okay?"

"I'm fine. Maybe a little tired. I'm not used to partying like we did last night."

"Got all rowdy, huh?"

"Maybe a little."

"What are you two talking about down there? You need to share with the class." Chrissy had an excellent knack of interrupting at the most opportune times. It's like she saw and heard everything. Probably what made her a good analyst.

"I was trying to get Miranda to share about your girl's night festivities, but she is being tight-mouthed."

"Good. That's how it is, kiddo. Whatever happens on girl's night stays secret."

"Got it."

"So don't try plying her for information, Miranda knows how to keep secrets."

They had no idea of the secrets Miranda knew and would never share, mostly about her father, but that was the whole point of secrets wasn't it.

"It's not a big deal."

"It is, secrets are important, Sunshine, and I'll always respect yours."

"Thank you, Cam."

"He knows all about secrets, we live them every day," Ryan said. It was the first thing he'd said since he greeted them when they arrived. Rafe had been right about him being quiet and eating. It was amazing just how much the three SEALs managed to eat in one sitting.

"It must be hard sometimes, not being able to talk about what you do. But I learned all about that with my dad."

"I didn't realize senators had many secrets, but I guess I should have," Ryan responded as he ate the last bite of food on his plate.

"Yeah." She didn't mention his prior work for the CIA and how most of her life had been based on his secrets. It was time to change the subject. "I'm curious, do they not feed you when you're on missions?"

"What? Of course they feed us. Depending on what we're doing it could be MREs. You had a few when you were with us, remember?" Cam said as he finished his plate.

"Oh yeah, I'll never forget that gourmet experience."

The men chuckled. Everyone at the table with the exception of Chrissy had experienced the joy of the MRE. The woman was lucky she'd avoided that pleasure.

"So I guess that's why you're always hungry?"

"We burn a lot of calories. Even when we're not working we're working out, staying on top of things."

"I hadn't thought about that. Maybe I need to add more than just yoga to my workout schedule."

Cam leaned over and whispered into her ear, "I wouldn't change a thing." Miranda could feel the heat creeping up her cheeks. If her mother had been there she'd have been mortified, but she was more comfortable around all of these new friends than her family and didn't care. That made her think of her mother and the text message and voicemails she hadn't answered. Shit. Then again, if there had been an actual problem, she would have called again.

As if she'd triggered it with her thoughts, her phone rang. She didn't have to guess it was her mother. The only other people she heard from were Meghan's brother Charlie, and Cam. It wouldn't be either of them, so that left her mother.

"I'm sorry, I need to take this. I'll just step outside." She grabbed her purse and answered the phone as she made her way between the tables and stepped outside.

"Mom?"

"Thank God. Why haven't you answered your phone or messages, Miranda? You had me worried sick." The first response she thought of would not be acceptable to Cherise Stanhope.

"I'm sorry. I let you know I got here okay. Then I was just hanging out with Meghan and Chrissy. I left my phone charging in the other room and didn't see your messages until a bit ago."

"That's not acceptable young lady. You know better."

"Yes, ma'am. I'm sorry. Is everything okay? Did something happen?"

"Everything is fine except for not hearing from you."

"Mom, I'm not twelve. You need to lighten up a bit."

"But you're my baby girl. You'll always be my baby girl. And you were almost killed." And there was the crux of the problem. Miranda wasn't sure if her mother would ever get over the fact she'd been taken hostage. But in order for Miranda to move past it, she needed her mother to as well.

"I know, but I'm fine. I'm with friends and three Navy SEALs. I don't think I can get much safer than that."

"I don't know…"

"I do, Mom. I'm okay." Cam startled the crap out of her when he came up behind her and put his hand on the small of her back. It shouldn't have freaked her out, but since she hadn't heard him approach it triggered a fight or flight response and she brought her heel down hard on his instep. Those self-defense classes had come in handy. Except it was Cam. Thank goodness he was wearing his heavy boots.

"What was that? Are you okay?"

"Yes, Mom. Cam just came out to check on me. See you have nothing to worry about. I bet I can't go to the bathroom without someone checking on me."

"Nothing wrong with that."

"Mother."

"Okay, I'll admit maybe that was a bit over the top. But I couldn't talk to your father. He was with the president yesterday and you weren't answering your phone. So, I just kind of panicked."

Hearing the worry and sadness in her mother's voice made Miranda feel guilty, and her mom was good at making her feel that way. She'd had many years of practice, but this time, she wasn't going to give in to it.

"I'm sorry, Mom. But I'm sure dad is fine and I'm fine. I'll call or text you tomorrow. Try to have a good day. Don't you have a garden club meeting or something?"

"No that's not until tomorrow. But I'll find something to do."

"Good. I love you. Bye."

"I love you too, Miranda."

"Wow, is she always like that?" Cam asked as she tucked the phone into her bag.

"Unfortunately, yes. Although, she's gotten ten times worse since the incident."

"The incident? You mean your abduction in Afghanistan?"

"Yes. She doesn't like to say it out loud, so it's become 'the incident' in our house."

"Got it, good thing you told me in case I decide to bring it up as a topic of conversation at dinner." Miranda smacked him in the stomach and laughed.

"And that reminds me, where did you learn that trick with your heel? You could have done some serious damage to me."

"I know, isn't it great? I've been taking self-defense classes. I was hoping it would help me feel better about going back to help finish the school there."

"Wait. When did you decide about going back? I thought you were still thinking about it."

"I was. But after talking to Charlie, I felt guilty about not wanting to go. So I started the classes to help."

"But they didn't?"

"No, but we can talk about it later. We should get back to the others."

"Okay, but first, I've been dying for one of your kisses." Before she could answer, he leaned down and took her lips in a gentle kiss, his lips barely moved against hers. But it didn't matter, it still triggered the same tingle she always got from his touch.

When he pulled back, Miranda sighed with happiness and received a huge bright smile in response.

"Ready?"

She never had a chance to answer. Instead, a hail of bullets rang out all around them. Before she could react she was down on the ground with Cam covering her with his body. The gunfire was so loud, echoing off the buildings and bits of brick flew through the air where the bullets impacted.

Finally, the shots stopped, and a car roared down the street with squealing tires. It didn't last long, but while she was lying there it seemed like forever. Terror, unlike anything she'd felt since the Middle East had paralyzed her with fear.

"Sunshine, are you okay?" Cam asked as he kneeled next to her on the concrete sidewalk.

"I think so. I don't understand. Were they shooting at us?"

"Not sure, but we'll find out. Here let me help you get up." Her heart was still racing a million miles an hour and she was shaking like a leaf. If he hadn't helped her she'd be lying on the side-walk for a long while.

"You've got blood on your face, are you sure you're not hurt?"

"I do?" Miranda reached up to touch her cheek. Feeling the stickiness she looked at her fingers. It was blood.

By then their friends surrounded them on the sidewalk, and Meghan handed her a tissue.

"It looks like it's from pieces of the brick that splintered off," Cam said as he took the tissue from her hand. "Let me do it."

He was so gentle with her like he'd been before, and it brought tears to her eyes. A chill traveled down her spine and she shook. Cam's eyes were filled with concern as he tended to the little scratches on her face. They didn't hurt and were nothing much at all, but it was the shock of the shooting that had freaked her out.

SOMEONE MUST HAVE HEARD THE SHOTS AND called the police. Sirens could be heard in the distance and the whining sound grew louder as they approached. Miranda shook in Cam's arms as he tried to soothe her fear.

The entire incident was surreal. So many questions swirled in his head. Who would open fire on them? Who even knew they were there? Was it him or Miranda that was the target? Or was it just a random shooting? Not that it mattered at the moment. All he wanted was to get his woman to a place that was safe and comfort her.

Rafe was on the phone with Jake, who would call the captain. The local police would handle the investigation. They were SEALs, not law enforcement, but it was standard operating procedure to notify their commanding officer when incidents involving law enforcement occurred.

"We should take the women inside. Get them off the street in case the fuckers come back."

"I agree," Rafe said after he ended his call. "Jake's calling Captain Knox and Murph since he's the only one not here."

"Murph will show up any minute now." No sooner had Ryan said the words, a black Harley roared to a stop across the street. "Told you. I guess I should have bet you on this one."

"Who's betting now? And what the fuck? Can't you guys go anywhere without being the center of attention?" Murph said with one of his shit-eating grins on his face. Talk about being the center of attention.

Rafe rolled his eyes and flipped him the bird over Meghan's head. It summed up how Cam felt too.

"Everyone's safe, thanks for asking, dickhead," Ryan responded.

"I knew that already, Jake told me. So don't go getting your panties in a twist. Oh, and thanks for inviting me to the party."

"It wasn't a party. There was no food in the house, and we needed to eat."

"And? I live right down the street."

"For fuck's sake, really?" Rafe replied.

At first, Murph was pissing him off, then he realized that all his carrying on had distracted Miranda and the other women too. She was no longer shaking and just leaning against him and her breathing had returned to normal.

The police pulled up a moment later and took over. First, they separated everyone, which pissed off Cam. He didn't want Miranda to be alone, but when they found out who she was, they offered to let her go inside and relax until they were ready to take her statement. They even let the other women accompany her.

The cop that spoke to Cam was young and likely a recent graduate from the Academy. It made him feel old, not that there was so a huge difference in age between them, but they were worlds apart in experience.

Cam gave his statement, which wasn't much. The car had been a black late model sedan, but he couldn't tell him the make or specific model. The license plate was covered so no tag numbers to work with either. That didn't leave much except for the bullets and casings the Crime Scene techs were collecting.

"Did you see how many people were discharging their firearms?"

"Not for sure. I heard the bullets before I saw anything and pulled Ms. Stanhope to the ground to protect her. When I looked up the car was already driving away. The passenger side windows were down, so I guess there were at least two shooters."

"Can you think of any reason why someone would shoot at you or Ms. Stanhope?"

"No, I just returned from a three-month deployment. Ms. Stanhope is visiting from Georgia. It makes me think it has nothing to do with us and maybe it's just the neighborhood."

"We don't have a lot of drive-by shootings in this area."

"There's a first time for everything."

"Maybe. Will you be in town for a while?"

"Unless I get a mission. My commanding officer has all my information and will know how to locate me, or my teammates should something come up."

"Okay. The detective assigned to the case may have more questions, but you're free to go."

"Thanks. What about the others?"

"I'll check but I think we've gotten all we need right now. Thank you for your cooperation."

Cam mumbled under his breath about not having a choice and he was sure the officer heard him, but wisely didn't say anything. This was some fucked up shit. They'd just gotten in a few hours ago. And Miranda? She didn't even live in the state. Didn't know this restaurant. They couldn't be the targets.

Cam walked over to where Rafe, Ryan, and Murph were talking. He and Miranda were the actual witnesses, so they'd been questioned the longest. Although he had a feeling they'd be going through the whole thing again with whoever was assigned the case.

"Any ideas what the fuck is going on?" he asked as he reached his teammates.

"Not a damn thing. We were hoping you had a clue."

"I think it has to do with the neighborhood or the restaurant. Maybe a grudge or something. We should talk to Phil, see if anyone's been giving him any trouble."

"That's an idea, but not right now. If the police think we're interfering in their investigation it will be a major clusterfuck. I can hear the captain now."

Murph laughed. "No shit. So now what? We all just go home and carry on?"

"I'm up for that. But I don't think the girls finished eating."

"Maybe not, but I doubt any of them would want to eat anything now."

"We can go back to my place," Rafe said.

"We have to pick up Halo and Miranda needs to get her bags, so we have to stop over but doubt we'll stay. I'll see if Chrissy can drive us over and then drop us at my place."

"I'm sure she will." Rafe nodded

"If she can't I'll take you," Ryan said.

"Thanks, appreciate it. I guess we need to get our women."

"Your women, I don't have a woman in there and neither does Murph," Ryan said with a grin.

"That's your fault," Rafe replied.

"What?"

"You're sitting on your ass instead of asking Chrissy out. We can see how you look at her. You're not fooling anyone."

"You're so full of shit. You better go get your woman before you can't walk. I don't think Meghan would appreciate it much."

"What won't I appreciate?"

"Go ahead and explain it, Ryan." They laughed as the color drained from Ryan's face. He was definitely the most sensitive of the team. It made up for Murph's usual assholeness.

"It's nothing. We're just joking around."

Meghan raised an eyebrow, but she left it alone. "So, we've been deemed free to go. I don't know about the rest of you, but I'm ready to leave this shit storm and go home. I could use a nap."

"A nap, huh?" Chrissy said with a giggle. "I just bet you can."

"Is nap code for a bit of bam-bam in the ham," Murph asked. Cam snorted when Rafe punched him. The rest of them tried to ignore him.

"Hey, Chrissy, can you give us a ride to Meghan's? We need to get Halo and I need to get my bags then drop us all off at Cam's? I know it's a lot of extra driving..." Cam wondered how much of their conversation the women had overheard, or if Miranda just had the same idea. Either way, he was ready to see the last of his team for a few hours.

"No problem, Miranda. Let's hit the road.

CHAPTER 8

BY THE TIME CHRISSY DROPPED THEM OFF IN front of Cam's apartment building, Miranda was ready for a nap. It had been a rollercoaster of emotions since he'd walked through the door of Meghan and Rafe's condo. The nightmare the night before hadn't helped either.

When she'd dreamed about their first time it had been all candlelight, soft music, wine and making love all night long. The reality was she was exhausted and could barely stand up, there was no way she'd survive a night of lovemaking. Not exactly the best girlfriend material. They'd decided to wait until she was healed so she wouldn't have to worry about being careful or reinjuring herself. Now that they were together and she was healthy, she was dead on her feet.

"You okay, Sunshine?" Cam asked as they

took the elevator up to the third floor. She wanted to kiss him for not taking the stairs. "This isn't quite what I planned for our first day."

"Me either. But at least it hasn't been boring."

"Very true." Halo woofed to add his two cents.

"You're a good boy," Miranda said as she patted his head. He'd been the first one to get to her in the cave and stayed by her side until help came. She'd always think of him as her doggy knight in shining armor.

"Here we are. Just down the hall and to the left. Number 3D." Cam carried both of their bags. All she did was follow along behind him. Halo stayed between them like he wasn't sure who needed him most. "Before you go in, it's not like Meghan and Rafe's place. It's a lot smaller."

"Size doesn't matter."

"Oh baby, you're going to change your tune later." Miranda realized what she'd said and turned scarlet. She walked right into that one.

"I don't care if your apartment is huge or not. Does it have a bedroom, bathroom, and kitchen?"

"Of course."

"Then that's all that matters. Seriously, just because you know where I grew up doesn't mean a thing."

"Okay." It was cute that he was worried, but material things never mattered to her. Besides, when she was young they didn't have all that stuff.

Her father needed them to blend in with everyone else.

After he unlocked the door, Halo was the first one into the apartment. Cam didn't even have to tell him to check it out, it was what he did. After Halo came back with the all clear, Cam led Miranda inside. He was right it was small, but he'd done a great job decorating. The furniture was definitely geared toward a bachelor, leather, glass, and wood, but it was clean, and that was the important part.

"So, what do you think?"

"I like it. It is definitely you."

"You think?"

"Yeah. Did you decorate it?"

"No, my sister did. She's an interior designer. When I passed BUD/S it was her present to me."

"She did great."

"The kitchen is over there but we'll have to do some shopping. There's not much in the fridge. The bedrooms are down here." He led the way down a short hallway with three doors. "There are two, but the second one is full of junk. I can sleep on the couch if you'll be more comfortable. There's just the one bathroom and it's through that door."

"I think we'll manage. You forget I lived with a missionary group in Afghanistan for almost four months. Outdoor bathrooms, tents, dirt. Your apartment is like the Ritz. Thank you for inviting me to stay."

"Sunshine, I've dreamed of having you here with me for months." She melted a little inside at his words and all the awkwardness and exhaustion melted too. Standing on her tip-toes, she pulled his face down and kissed him. His lips were so warm and soft, probably the only soft part on her warrior.

"You are magical, Cam Patterson. You've turned this woman into a melted puddle of goo."

"Oh no. Goo? Not sure that's a good thing."

"Oh baby, it's the best thing."

~

BEFORE SHE HAD A CHANCE TO CHANGE HER mind, he slipped one arm under her knees and the other around her back and lifted her into his arms. "You mean the world to me, Sunshine. I've dreamed of this moment in my long lonely nights in the desert. If you don't want this tell me now."

He held his breath while he waited for her answer. Either way, he wouldn't put her down until he reached his bed. The question would be whether he climbed into it with her or left her to get some rest and took a cold shower.

"I want this..."

The words were soft, husky, and barely audible, but she'd said them. It was all he could do not to 'yee-haw' as he pushed through the slightly open bedroom door. This was one room he'd decorated on his own from the king-sized bed to the black lacquer furniture and white carpet.

Although he was tempted to toss her on the bed, he resisted, and placed her gently on the edge, and knelt down in front of her.

"What are you doing?"

"Undressing you. You're the present I've been waiting for and I'm going to take my time unwrapping you."

"But...wouldn't you rather we just got under the covers and..."

"No, baby. I've been imagining this moment for so long." When he saw the indecision on her face he tried to figure out what he'd done wrong. Just a minute ago she seemed to want this as much as him. "What's wrong? Would you rather wait until tomorrow?"

"It's not that. I'm just worried about what you'll think of my body when you see it. The scars."

Cam got up and sat down next to her on the bed. Then he took her hand and weaved her fingers between his. "Miranda, maybe I haven't said this enough or at all, but you are amazing from your head to your toes. There is nothing about you that will bother me, except if you walk away."

"Really?"

"Your scars are like medals of honor for surviving, how could I think that is ugly, or whatever else you might think."

"I don't know. I just, maybe I'm being silly. I know I'm not a perfect woman, but the scars are still so new, and I think they're ugly…"

"Well, I disagree with you. And I always will if you say things like that about yourself."

Halo picked that time to jump onto the bed. Cam hadn't thought about that part since he'd never brought a woman back to his place before. Talk about awkward. No way was he having Halo watch his every move as they had sex. That would be a big hell no.

Halo scooted next to Miranda and as she rubbed his head he got the same look on his face that Cam did when she kissed him. Good grief, they both were hooked on her.

"I think we'll wait until tomorrow. Today's been fucked up and scary for you. How about we watch a movie and just relax. I'll run out and get some stuff from the store and you can take a shower and change. I'll leave Halo to protect you."

"You don't mind waiting?"

"Sunshine, I'll wait forever if I have to." Then

he lifted the hand that was intertwined with his and kissed each of her fingers and then the back of her hand. "You will always be worth waiting for."

Tears welled up in Miranda's eyes which was not the effect he'd been going for and he wasn't sure what to do. Pulling her closer he wrapped his arms around her and just held her while she cried. Fuck, he was a shit head. He thought he was doing a good thing.

"I'm so sorry. I didn't mean to make you cry."

"No, oh no. It's not that. You are like some hero out of a book. You're sweet, kind, protective, understanding. I wonder how you could be real. You're right today sucked, and I'm freaked out. But none of it is because of you."

"Trust me, you will find out I'm not so wonderful when you spend more time with me. Ask any of the guys if you don't believe me."

This time she did what he'd hoped, she grinned and then started giggling. It was the shock wearing off, but he didn't care. He'd give his right testicle to keep her happy.

"Thank you, Cam."

"For?"

"Being you and caring about me." She had no idea just how much he cared, but she'd find out. And hopefully, it wouldn't send her running for home.

"My pleasure." Dropping a kiss on her forehead, he stood up and lifted her off the bed. "Do you want anything special while I'm out? Anything you like to eat for breakfast, snacks, middle of the night binges?"

"People do that?"

"Oh yeah. Murph had one girl he was with a couple of times and she didn't eat all day or when he took her to dinner. In the middle of the night, he woke up and she wasn't in bed."

"Where was she?"

"In the kitchen, standing there eating everything in sight. He was freaked out."

"What did he do?"

"Went back to bed. Figured it wasn't his place to say anything, but when she left the next day he slipped her the card for the therapist they recommend for us."

"Wow. I hope she's okay."

"Don't know, none of us ever saw her again. So, do you have a wish list from the grocery store, my Princess?"

"Coffee, maybe some bread and fixings for omelets for breakfast. I don't eat a lot of snacks, so get whatever you like. Although popcorn works for the movie."

"Soda?"

"Nope, I'm a coffee, water, or wine type of woman."

"Okay. I'll be back soon. Don't open the door for anyone. Halo will be on protection detail, right boy?"

After another quick kiss, he forced himself to leave. It would be too easy to stay and keep kissing her, but he'd promised a quiet evening and that's what she'd get. Technically it wasn't even late, but after the day she'd had he wouldn't be surprised if she was asleep when he returned.

Cam had just climbed into his truck and closed the door when his cell rang. Figuring it was Miranda with something she'd thought of, he answered without looking at the caller ID.

"Hey, Sunshine did you forget something?"

"No, turd blossom, but thanks for asking."

"Fuck you, Murph. Didn't we see enough of each other earlier?"

"Yeah, but I'm just checking on you. That shooting doesn't feel right, and we wanted to make sure you were okay."

"Why wouldn't I be? I've got Halo and I am a SEAL. I think I could handle most things that came my way."

"Knock that chip off your shoulder, kid. It's serious. Jake has us all on alert. He's got one of those feelings."

"Fuck."

"So keep an eye out and if anything is weird,

call one or all of us. And make sure you have your phone near in case we call."

"Copy that. I'm headed to the store and I left Miranda in the apartment, but Halo is with her. Maybe I shouldn't go."

"She'll be fine especially with Halo there. We don't think it involves her, that it's us they're after."

Fuck. So much for some peaceful time off. It never fucking failed. "Gotcha. Thanks for letting me know."

Jake's 'feelings' were never good and usually on point. It was like some freaky antenna that he had. Hopefully, this would be the first time he was wrong. Even so, he stayed extra vigilant as he drove to the store and while he grabbed the items on his list. He wasn't sure if someone was watching him or if it was his imagination, but the little hairs on the back of his neck stood up as he headed back to the truck. Loading everything into the passenger side gave him a chance to look around. Nothing seemed off, but he couldn't shake the feeling that someone had their eyes on him.

Cam made it back home in less than an hour. When he opened the door, he was relieved and a little surprised to see Miranda sitting on the couch watching TV with Halo by her side.

They both looked toward the door when he came in. "Do you need any help?"

"Nope, I've got it. Any trouble?"

"Only if you consider Halo trying to hang out in the bathroom with me while I showered. I told him that he wasn't allowed, and he wasn't happy."

Laughing, Cam put away the groceries. "Good dog. I told him to stay by your side, so he was following orders. Orders are important."

"I know, but did you expect him to be in the bathroom with me?"

"I wanted him to be there if you needed him, but no. I didn't expect him to hang out in the bathroom, but I'm not surprised."

"Next time you'd better be more specific then."

"There won't be a next time."

"Why not?"

"Because I won't be leaving you alone again while you're here. Can you blame me for wanting to spend as much time as possible with you?" Hopefully, he'd be forgiven for his sort of white lie. He did want to spend as much time as possible, but he wouldn't take the chance of leaving her alone again either.

"I like that idea. I know the week is going to fly by." She was right about that. The good times always passed too quickly.

Filling a bowl with popcorn, he grabbed a beer for him and a bottle of water for her and joined her on the couch. Halo didn't want to move so Miranda ended up in the middle between her two overly protective men. But from the smile on her face, he didn't think she minded at all.

After much discussion, they settled on the first Captain America movie since it had action and a great love story, even if it didn't have a happy ending. As Cam expected, about halfway through the movie, Miranda was asleep on his shoulder. It reminded him of when he was growing up, how his mom would fall asleep on his dad. The warmth of the memory lifted some of the worry that had worn on him since Murph's call.

CHAPTER 9

IT WAS DARK WHEN MIRANDA WOKE UP screaming. But this time she wasn't alone, Cam held her in his arms and rocked her.

"Easy, Sunshine. It's just a dream. You're safe. I have you."

"I'm sorry." Her voice sounded hoarse and tearful. Two nights in a row hadn't happened in ages. The shooting earlier on top of all the other stresses didn't help.

"You have nothing to be sorry about. I guess I don't have to ask if you're still having the nightmares."

"Not as often, but I had one last night at Meghan's."

"I know, she told me earlier. She's worried about you. So am I."

"They were getting better…"

"Why don't you want to see someone?"

"I don't know. I told myself I didn't want to dredge up all the memories. Talking about them makes it all fresh. But it seems like a stupid excuse. I think I'm just scared."

"I think it's something else. Something you're trying not to remember. You braved so much while they had you captive and survived."

Was he right? Was there something else she'd blocked from her time in captivity that she was afraid to remember? That made more sense than any other explanation, but it also scared the crap out of her. Everything she remembered was horrible, did she want to remember something that was even worse.

"Maybe that's it. But if that's the reason, I'm not sure I want to remember."

"But if you can work through that, maybe the nightmares will stop." He had a point, but she needed to not think about it anymore, at least not right then.

"I'll think about it, but not right now. Okay?"

"I'm not trying to push you, Sunshine. I just want you to not be afraid anymore."

"Thank you. I'm sorry I woke you."

"It's an occupational hazard. Can I get you anything? Some cold water?"

"That would be great. I'm going to splash some cool water on my face." He kissed her before he let her go, and a little more of the terror evaporated.

Cam had a fresh bottle of water waiting for her when she returned, and he'd put the stereo on with some Paganini. That he'd remembered it was one of her favorite pieces surprised her.

"Thank you so much."

"You're welcome so much. Do you think you can go back to sleep or do you want to get up?"

"I think I'll be able to get back to sleep in a little bit. We can lie here and talk."

They settled into the bed and that's when she remembered she'd fallen asleep during the movie. He must have brought her in and put her to bed. After another swallow, she tucked herself against his side and listened to his heartbeat.

"What would you like to do tomorrow?"

"I don't care as long as I'm with you. But it might be fun to go to the beach."

"Beach it is. Did you bring a bathing suit, or do we need to go shopping first?"

"Oh, I'm not going into the water, besides I don't want to show my legs with all the scars."

"I thought we talked about this."

"Yeah but kids go to the beach, I don't want to scare them."

'Dammit, Miranda." Cam sighed and she felt bad. She didn't want to make a big deal about this, but she couldn't help it. Maybe she did need to go to counseling.

"I'm sorry. Maybe the beach wasn't a good idea."

"Sure it was. And we'll go, and you can dress any way you want to. But hopefully one of these days you'll realize you don't have to hide from the world."

"Thank you." She leaned up to kiss him, just a quick one on the lips, but when they touched the flames of passion she'd been keeping pushed down flared to life. He took control and rolled her onto her back. Balancing over her, as he lowered his head to take her lips again, she saw the sparkle of his eyes even in the dim light of the room.

Cam's tongue darted into her mouth, then sucked on her tongue, and the kiss grew more intense as he leaned against her and his hard-on made it clear that he wanted her.

She groaned and arched against him her legs captured between his. Pulling away they were both gasping for air. She'd never been so turned on by a kiss. He'd aroused every inch of her body and it craved his touch.

"I need you, Cam."

"Are you sure, baby? We agreed to wait until tomorrow. But if we keep this up, I'm not sure I can stop."

"I'm sure." Worried that he'd pull away, she

sat up and pulled her sleep shirt over her head and leaned on the pillows beneath him. He swore just loud enough for her to hear him, and at first, she thought it was about the scars, but he must have seen the look on her face.

"You're fuckin' gorgeous. For the love of all things holy, you have no idea do you?"

"I don't know."

"I'll just have to show you." Not sure what he meant, having him get off the bed was the last thing she expected. But it was just long enough to strip out of his t-shirt and boxers. Then it was her turn to stare at him. The moon had to be full, otherwise, the light shining through the mini-blinds were divine intervention. His body was illuminated as he stood beside the bed, glowing like an angel.

She couldn't look away, wondering if maybe all of this was a dream. Until he climbed on the bed and pulled off her panties. He slid over her body and balanced on his elbows to make sure he didn't put all his weight on her. There was nothing soft about Cam, and when his hard-on twitched against her, she arched her back and made him groan.

"If you keep that up, I won't last long, and I want to make this special for you."

"It already is."

"Ahh, Sunshine, you have no idea." He was

right, she didn't but she had no doubt that she'd found the perfect man for the job.

~

REPEATING OVER AND OVER IN HIS HEAD THAT he needed to move slowly so he wouldn't scare her, helped to calm his raging need. When she'd removed her shirt, he thought he was going to come just from seeing her lying there, bathed in the light of the full moon and all his. He'd dreamed of that moment for months, and it was even better than his best fantasy. Now he had to make sure it was for her too.

The sight of her glorious breasts whet his appetite for a taste. Sliding his tongue across her already taut nipple, it grew even harder. As he continued to lick and tease it with his teeth, he massaged the other breast. Focusing on her pleasure, her writhing underneath him was all the encouragement he needed.

It might just about kill him, but he wanted all of her memories of their first night to be amazing. Each time she rubbed against his hard cock was like sweet torture but reciting mission checkpoints in his head, helped to maintain his control.

Learning what made her moan the loudest was a course he looked forward to taking for a long time to come. But for Miranda 101, he learned that her breasts were extra sensitive and even the slightest touch of his tongue elicited a response. But when he sucked it into his mouth and nibbled with his teeth, she came apart in his arms. She writhed against him and moaned his name over and over, begging him for more.

Every inch of her required the same attention but there was no way he could restrain himself this first time. But it didn't mean he couldn't try. Slowly he worked his way down her body. He licked and kissed each scar he came across. This was the first time seeing her undressed, and he understood better why she was so concerned. He'd had no idea they'd carved her up from her breasts to her knees. He'd seen much worse, but it angered him to know how much she'd suffered.

"It's not your fault. You stopped it before it got worse."

It was like she could read his mind. "I know, and it's not what you think. They don't disgust me. They are part of you, help to make you the woman you are, and I wouldn't change anything."

"Ahh, Cam…" He'd wanted her to stop thinking and sliding his tongue along her lower lips did the trick. Focusing on the bundle of nerves, circling it with his tongue before sucking it between his teeth.

"Oh my God, oh God," she whispered. Shuddering beneath him as she found her release. But he didn't stop, just kept up the licking, sucking, and then inserted a finger into her slick passage. She was already wet and ready for him, but he wanted more for her first.

Thrusting first one then two fingers into her, he worked to stretch and searched for her G-spot. He was a big boy, and she was tight. The last thing he wanted was to hurt her, but he needed to be buried deep inside her as much as she was begging him to be there. Her muscles clenched around his fingers so hard they almost cut off the circulation, the spasming increased and just when he thought she was on the edge he bit down gently on her clit.

No whispering this time. She screamed his name loud enough the neighbors would definitely be giving him the side eye. It made him smile, as he licked her juices and hoped it would be the first of many mind-blowing orgasms.

After he'd licked her clean, he moved up the bed and stretched out next to her. Then he pulled her up on top of him with his cock settled between her legs. It was his turn to twitch and moan.

"Why did you stop? Aren't you going to have sex with me?" she'd said it so softly at first he wasn't sure he'd heard her.

"Yes, Sunshine, we are most definitely. But I thought you might like to be in control this first time."

"I've never done it this way."

"No worries, you'll get the hang of it. It's better for the woman in this position."

"Better than what you already did? I might die."

"I promise you that this is only the beginning and none of this will kill you except with pleasure."

"A little sure of yourself?"

"Maybe. I'll let you be the judge. Now, how about you start with a kiss unless you mind your taste?"

She hesitated and he wondered if maybe it was something else she hadn't tried, but then she eased up his body and kissed him. And not some shy touch of the lips, she gave him back everything he'd given her, sliding her tongue between his lips and sucking on his, moaning as her desire amped up again.

For a brief moment, Cam wondered if this hadn't been such a good idea. He was going to lose it before she even took him inside. Breaking the kiss, she slid down his chest, then took his nipple in her mouth, repeating everything he'd done to her, licking, sucking and then nibbling until he moaned and couldn't keep his hips still.

"Sunshine, my restraint is wearing thin. If you don't want me to come before I'm inside you, you need to stop."

With a look of pure female satisfaction that curled his toes, she moved further down his body, but instead of shifting to take him inside, she slid her kiss-swollen lips over his rigid shaft.

"You don't…"

"Yes, I do. I let you do what you want, this is my turn."

His brain turned to mush, this was not what he'd expected, but fuck it was incredible. Her mouth was so hot and what she did with her tongue and teeth, eroded what was left of his will power and he came. He tried to pull out of her mouth, but she held on, taking all he had to give.

"Fuck. Miranda, I don't even know what to say."

"How about, that was amazing?"

"It was that. But damn, woman. When I put you on top it wasn't for that."

"But you liked it, right?"

"Fuck yes. But I wanted to be inside you."

"I didn't realize we were done yet. You're still rock hard, baby."

"Fuck. Maybe I was wrong, maybe you can die from sex." Then he pulled her face to his and kissed her with all the feelings he hadn't been able to say out loud.

"Now, where were we?" She settled over him and slid down his hard cock one throbbing inch at a time. He couldn't have answered her if his life depended on it. He'd been worried about shocking her with his skills, but she'd knocked him sideways.

Cam was large and even if she was skilled, it would be a lot to take since it was her first time in a while. He'd tried to stretch her with his fingers, but she was making it difficult. Trying to ease in and slow down, he held onto her hips and arched up as she slid down his shaft. Sweat dotted his brow as he struggled for control. She was so hot, tight and wet.

"Relax, baby. Slowly…" She listened, and her clenched muscles loosened around him. Seated fully inside, her muscles spasmed around his shaft. Slowly, she started the rhythm, it was like sweet torture, as she slid all the way up his cock and down. Over and over, until he couldn't take it anymore.

Flipping them over so she was on her back, he smiled at her shocked expression. "Sorry, Sunshine, but I just can't hold back."

Rubbing her clit as he thrust inside her faster and faster, she quivered and writhed, but he held back until her orgasm started. Then he thrust hard and fast until his body quaked with his release.

Cam didn't want to move, wanted them both to stay just as they were. Capturing the moment in his memory to hold on to, the look on her face, seeing her hair spread all over his pillows in every direction, the red marks on her chest from his day-old beard, and finally her flavor.

"Wow," Miranda said with a sigh as she stared into his eyes.

"Yes, it was. Incredible. You're amazing."

"If I am, it's your fault."

"I think it's always been inside you, just waiting for the right person to wake it up."

"Maybe. But if all my nightmares are cured this way, I'm not sure I'll mind them as much."

Cam laughed. "Just think how much better it would be if it hadn't started with you terrified. I'll be right back. I'm going to get a towel and some cold water for you."

"You…"

"Shh. Just relax, Sunshine, and let me do this."

It had taken every ounce of restraint not to say, 'I love you,' but he didn't think she was ready to hear the words yet. It surprised him that he was ready to say them. They'd known each other over six months but most of that time they'd been apart. Skype and text messages, phone calls, none of that was the same, but he knew what his heart wanted. Now it was just a matter of proving to her that she was his one and only passion.

CHAPTER 10

MIRANDA WOKE UP TO HOT BREATH AND LICKS. As she slowly opened her eyes, she came face-to-face with Halo who was grinning and wagging his tail.

"Are you my wakeup call?"

"Woof." The one word delivered gently as if he understood what she'd asked.

"Where's Cam?" Halo jumped off the bed and left the room, making her laugh.

Sitting up against the pillows, she finger-combed her hair and thought about last night. Her cheeks grew warm just thinking about how ballsy she'd been. He'd said that maybe she just needed the right person. It sure seemed to be that way.

Jeremiah, her boyfriend in college had begged her to be more aggressive, but he was just 'meh.'

Probably 'bagging' a senator's daughter was a notch on his belt. He figured they'd get married, but there was no way in hell that was going to happen. The first thing she'd done after graduation was to break up with him. Sometimes she wondered if that had been her real motivation for joining the Deliver Hope Ministries. It had certainly gotten her out of his circle.

While she was still contemplating that earlier decision, Halo came back dragging Cam with him.

"You called, Sunshine? I'd hoped you were going to sleep in."

"Then you need to have a word with our furry friend, here. He was breathing on my face and licking me. I thought it was you, then I realized the breath was better."

"What?" He jumped on the bed, laughing, and grabbed one of the other pillows and smacked her on top of the head. Nothing hard and it cracked her up. Reaching behind her she got up on her knees and they had a full-fledged pillow fight until one of them split, and sent feathers flying everywhere.

Halo ran back and forth at the end of the bed, barking and jumping for the floating feathers. When he'd decided he'd been left out long enough he jumped onto the bed and tackled Cam.

It was the funniest thing Miranda had seen in

a long time. Dog and handler were covered in white feathers and the dog had Cam pinned. Every time he barked, the feathers would be disturbed and float back into the air. She was laughing so hard that she could barely breathe. Her stomach muscles cramped, and she fell onto her side next to Cam, still giggling.

Halo leaned over and licked her face. It made her laugh even harder and sputter when his tongue slipped into her mouth. "Ugh, gross, Halo. You're as bad as Cam. Always trying to get your tongue in my mouth."

"Except you like mine," Cam said and waggled his eyebrows. She couldn't disagree with that. She needed to brush her teeth so she could have another one of those toe-curling kisses.

"I'll be right back. And keep that dog out of the bathroom."

"Yes, ma'am. Would you like some coffee?"

"Oh, yeah. That would be wonderful."

"Here or in the kitchen?"

"Kitchen might be a better idea. I don't like feathers in my coffee."

"Good point."

Brushing her teeth, turned into a shower and washing her hair. It helped ease some of the soreness from yesterday. She wasn't sure whether it was more from hitting the hard sidewalk or the busy night in bed. Probably the nighttime lovemaking session, she was already looking forward to the next time. Just thinking about it made her wet. She half-hoped he'd get tired waiting for her and join her in the shower.

Then she realized what she'd said. Yesterday she was worried about him seeing her naked body and all the scars and today she wanted him in the shower with her. After drying off, she wiped down the mirror to take a good look at herself. Most of the scars were on her belly and down her legs, they were angry, red, ragged and some of them still looked unhealed. Not a pretty site at all, but after the way Cam had treated her last night, she didn't look at them the same way.

"Are you almost done, or do I need to come in there and help you?"

Now he asks, so much for timing. "I'm just getting dressed, I'll be right out."

"Too bad."

Yeah, no kidding she said under her breath and then started giggling. Man one night of mind-blowing sex and she was a new woman. As she dragged a comb through her damp hair and added a touch of mascara, she wondered if she'd seem different to anyone else. Not that she cared, she liked this version of herself. But was it just the glow of last night? She wouldn't know until she had to go back to Georgia, and the thought of leaving Cam squeezed her heart.

Gathering her toiletries she put them back in her case and followed the aroma of coffee. Entering the kitchen, she was surprised to find the table set, a mug of coffee waiting for her, and Cam frying bacon. She was about to comment on it when she realized he was also on the phone.

Rather than interrupt she petted Halo on the head as she passed him and grabbed her coffee mug and went into the living room. A few moments later, Cam came to find her.

"Good morning, Sunshine. Again," he said over her shoulder. He'd startled her again, damn these guys were stealthy.

"Dang," she exclaimed as she almost spilled her coffee. "You have to stop sneaking up on me."

"Sorry, I'm not doing it on purpose."

"I know, it's okay. Good morning again," she answered with a huge smile. He grabbed the mug out of her hand and put it on the coffee table and then pulled her into his embrace.

"How about some sugar?"

"You already put it in my coffee."

"That's not what I meant. You are from the south aren't you?" Miranda laughed, she loved it when she could get him back.

"Yes, I am, bless your little heart." It was his turn to smile, and then he didn't wait for permission, just gave her the kiss she'd been hoping for.

He tasted like coffee and bacon and she wanted as much as she could get.

"Now that's more like it."

"I would have to agree with you on that."

"Breakfast is ready." He said as he picked up her mug and steered her into the kitchen.

"You didn't have to do all of this?"

"I wanted to. Besides, I'm starving. We never ate dinner last night."

"Oh yeah. I guess I fell asleep didn't I?"

"You needed it. I could have made something. As you can see, I'm perfectly capable of feeding myself."

"I guess you are." Besides the bacon, he'd made omelets and toast and hash brown potatoes. She sure hoped he was as hungry as he said because there was no way she was eating all of that.

"Do you need more coffee?"

"No, I'm fine. Thank you for making this amazing breakfast."

"Well, there might be a slight ulterior motive too."

"I was wondering about that. Something to do with that phone call?"

"Yes, but let's eat first and talk afterward. I am starving. You wouldn't want me to keel over from hunger, would you?"

"Ehh, I'm sure you'd survive," she replied with a giggle before taking a bite of bacon. Miranda had made it through about half of her omelet and eaten a few slices of the bacon when she was stuffed. Pushing the remainder of the food around her plate, she watched as Cam ate almost everything else. Where he put it, she had no idea. Maybe he had invisible pouches built into his body to store food for a rainy day? She'd never seen anyone eat so much in one sitting and not explode.

Miranda was waiting for him to bring up the phone call, but he held off while they cleared away breakfast and washed and put away all the dishes. They worked well together and made lots of small talk about the local area and the weather. It was odd, and obvious that he didn't want to talk about whatever he'd found out.

~

THERE WAS NOTHING ELSE TO DO, AND NO WAY to stall for more time. It's not like what he had to tell her was horrible, but it wasn't great either. The last thing he wanted was to disappoint her or wipe the bright smile from her face. But this was unavoidable.

"Let's talk in the living room. The couch is a lot more comfortable than these chairs. I don't know what my sister was thinking when she picked them out."

"That they looked perfect with the table."

"Maybe," he said with a smile. Miranda was coming out of her shell and he couldn't be happier. He believed a lot of it was just trying to always please her parents.

"My mother says it's always best to just rip the bandage off in one quick pull. It hurts but the pain is quickly over."

"What?"

"You're stalling, whatever it is you have to say, just tell me. It'll be okay unless you're dumping me. Then I might have to hurt you."

"I'm definitely not dumping you. I hope you weren't thinking that."

"No, but since you'd been stalling for so long I was starting to wonder."

"I'm sorry. You are amazing…" Before he could go on she rolled her eyes at him and made the motion to get on with it. Oh yeah, she was definitely coming out of her shell. "We got called into work today. Not a mission as far as I know. But I have to go to the base for a debriefing on yesterday's shooting. I don't think it will take too long."

"And that's what you were worried about telling me?"

"Well, yeah. You came to visit me and then

I'm almost two days late and now I have to go to work. It's not much fun for you."

"Cam, I understand. You don't have to worry about me. What time do you have to be there?"

"Soon, at eleven hundred hours."

"So what do I do? Stay here with Halo?"

"Not this time. Halo has to come with me, but I'm going to drop you off at Meghan's. She said you'd want to go shopping or something? With any luck by the time you are done, I'll be there to pick you up and we'll still have time to go to the beach."

"That sounds great. Meghan is okay with my barging in again?"

"Yup, Rafe said she suggested it."

"Okay, see, no worries. I like Meghan. I wish I'd known her when she lived in Atlanta and we could have hung out then. Both she and Chrissy are hysterical."

"And troublemakers. Don't let them corrupt you."

"No promises," she said and kissed him. "I'm going to grab my bag and phone and make sure my mom hasn't gone off the deep end again. Be right back."

Cam watched her walk down the hall then called his chief.

"Jake, any news?"

"No, nothing else but Tex is checking in to it.

He also said to let you know that the tracker you put on her phone is still working just fine."

"Good. I don't like letting her out of my sight when we don't know where the threat is coming from."

"Rafe feels the same way, but both of their trackers are hot. Tex will know where they are as long as they have their phones."

"Copy that. Miranda's getting ready and then I'll drop her at Meghan's and come in."

"Copy that." He'd just disconnected his call when Miranda appeared.

"Crisis averted."

"What crisis?"

"The one called Cherise Stanhope. She just sent the second text message. Next would have been the first of many phone calls, but I headed her off at the pass. Told her I was going out shopping and I'd call her later."

"You said she's been worse since you came back. But I didn't realize it was this bad."

"The abduction flipped a switch and she's way over the top now."

"Maybe she'll calm down when she realizes you're safe."

"You forget, I'm supposed to go back. When she finds that out she'll need to be sedated."

"Halo," Cam called then looked around to make sure the stove was off, and the coffeemaker was unplugged. It was a habit since he traveled so much. Then he led Miranda into the hallway and locked the door. "Are you committed to going back? I understand why you want to go, but I'm sure you could get out of it if you wanted to."

"Yes, I'm sure I could. But I feel like I need to do it for me. To prove that I've gotten over it."

"You don't have to prove anything to anyone, Sunshine."

"I know, but…"

"Seriously, you went through hell. No one would think less of you if you didn't go back. You can't tell me Charlie would give you a hard time."

"You're right. But I was thinking it would be like falling off a horse and getting back on and riding."

"If that's truly what you want then I'll back you one hundred percent but going through what you did isn't remotely close to falling off a horse. You are suffering from PTSD and it could get much worse if you go back."

"I didn't think about that. But I'm not sure I have PTSD."

"I've seen the symptoms, trust me, Sunshine, you do. Just promise you'll think about it a bit more before you make the final preparations."

"Okay, I promise."

They'd reached Cam's truck by then and he pushed the unlock button and opened the door.

Halo jumped in the backseat, then he helped Miranda into the passenger seat. Walking around the perimeter, he checked that nothing looked out of place and then hopped in.

"Are you shopping for anything specific?"

"No, I figured I'd pick up a few more things. It's more relaxed here so maybe a couple of t-shirts and a pair of sneakers. I didn't think to pack anything casual this time. I was too excited to see you."

Cam smiled. He understood the feeling. He'd been like a caged bear for the last week and had been surprised no one shot him to put him out of his misery.

They reached Meghan's a few minutes later and after he made sure Miranda was safe inside he headed to the base.

CHAPTER 11

As soon as Meghan closed the door, she turned around and laughed. "Woo hoo someone got laid last night. How was it?"

"What?" Miranda felt the color creep into her cheeks. Obviously, she had the answer to her question about looking different.

"Come on. You have that just fucked look and so did Cam. Are you going to tell me nothing happened?"

"Maybe," Miranda's cheeks were flaming based on how hot she felt. "Okay, yes we did, but I'm not going to tell you any details."

"It's okay. I wouldn't want you to. I'd never be able to look at Cam again without thinking about it." They both laughed, that would be horrible. No one should have that much information. "So what do you want to do for the next few hours?"

"Could we go shopping? Unless you have some other ideas?"

"We can start with shopping then grab some lunch and see what's what after that."

"Sounds great. Are you sure I'm not keeping you from anything?"

"It's the weekend. Rafe was supposed to be home so I didn't have any plans. But this happens all the time. That's the hard part of being in a relationship with a special operator."

"I'm figuring that out. But it was pretty much the same growing up with my dad."

"You mean him being away all the time?" Miranda had forgotten she hadn't told her about the CIA.

"It was hard because he was away for school plays, graduations, birthdays, so yeah. But I had Mom and she was always there. He was CIA for twenty years before he decided to get out and run for office. When he because a senator it was the same but different. He spends a lot of time in DC now and Mom didn't want to move there."

"I didn't realize. But okay, enough of this depressing stuff. Do you want to go to the mall or somewhere else?"

"Where's the best store for t-shirts and sneakers?"

"I know just the place."

Miranda had never been in a Target, but she

liked it. They had everything she wanted. After buying three new t-shirts and a couple of polos, she picked out a pair of sneakers. It was fun shopping with a girlfriend, although Meghan was a bad influence. She even talked her into trying on some bathing suits. That was the hardest part.

They went through all the racks looking for the perfect suit, but Miranda was convinced it didn't exist. Meghan kept pushing her and eventually, they found three one-piece suits that would cover all her scars except those on her legs.

"Cam didn't put you up to this did he?"

"Cam? No. Why would you ask that?"

"No reason. It's just that we had this discussion yesterday about bathing suits. It's a weird coincidence."

Meghan put her hand over her heart. "I promise. I never discussed bathing suits with Cam."

"Okay. I believe you. I think." Then ducked as Meghan tossed a swimsuit at her head.

"Are you going to try those on or get all of them?"

Holding up the three suits one at a time, she realized none of them were too bad. But she definitely didn't need three. "Try them on I guess."

"Yes. Good choice. The changing rooms are this way." She followed Meghan and got her little ticket thing then went in to try them on. "Don't forget to come out and show me."

Damn, what was she twelve? This part was like shopping with her mother. The last thing she wanted to do was model the swimsuit in the middle of a store full of people. Then she realized there wasn't much difference between the store and the beach.

"Yeah, yeah. Give me a few minutes."

In the tiny dressing room, she pulled off her clothes and tried the first one. It wasn't too bad. Black with white diagonal stripes from her left shoulder to her right hip. It didn't make her look like she was stuffed into the suit and she half liked it. With a sigh, she stepped outside to show Megan.

"Ohhh, I like that."

"Yeah?" Miranda was trying not to look down and see how much the scars were showing. "Be right back in the next one."

The second one was hideous. It hadn't looked bad on the hanger but on her body, holy crapola. It was a definite no and couldn't bear to step outside for anyone to see it. Quickly stripping off the horrific fabric, she grabbed her last choice.

"What's going on in there, everything okay?"

"Yeah, but the second suit was horrible. I skipped to number three."

It wouldn't have been her choice, it was a bright blue, sort of like the sky without clouds and the color did a reverse fade to dark navy following the same diagonal lines as the shoulder straps in front and back. It was pretty, simple, and the color was one of her favorites. But it was bright and would draw attention to her.

Opening the door, she showed Meghan, except it wasn't just her, Rafe and Cam were there too. She took a deep breath and told herself it was okay. If she was going to move forward with her life, then it had to be with all of it and not just the comfy parts.

"So, what do you think?"

Meghan clapped. "Oh yeah, this is it. It's gorgeous and makes your eyes pop. I mean the black one was nice, but this is the one. Sort of like saying "Yes to the Dress" but instead it's says, 'yes to the swimsuit.'"

Miranda smiled and took another deep breath before asking the others. "What to do you think?" Slowly she raised her eyes to Cam's. Her insecurity dissipated as soon as she saw the look on his face.

"You look gorgeous. I agree with Meghan. This is the color for you."

"Thank you." Rafe hadn't said anything but he was nodding his head as Cam spoke. Another obstacle overcome. Maybe she'd needed to visit before now, instead of always letting Cam come to Georgia. Being away from her parent's house was like freedom, even more so than being with the missionary group.

After changing into her clothes she grabbed her other choices and they checked out. Since the guys were back early, they went to lunch together.

"How about we go to the Mexican place down the street? I don't want to go back to the Ice House for a while." Meghan said.

"I agree. The food was great, but I'm not ready for more of the after meal entertainment," Miranda said, trying to make light of yesterday's shooting. They all smiled, but she caught the look Cam and Rafe exchanged and wondered if she'd find out what was going on.

~

THE TEAM WAS WITH CAPTAIN KNOX IN THE conference room by the time Cam and Halo arrived. He didn't like the solemn look on everyone's faces, and the fact that even Murph didn't make asshole remark about him being late wasn't a good sign.

After he took his place at the table, Jake and the captain filled him in on what they'd found out about the shooter.

"We don't have an ID yet, but we have a few leads and it looks like they were after us, not

Miranda. But now that they know she's here, that could change."

"Why are they after us?"

"Chatter has turned up some weird information."

"Why isn't Lynch here then?" The CIA was the purveyor of that information and since he was embedded with their team, he was the one who shared the updates.

"Because he wasn't the one who picked it up. I think you all know Chrissy Stillwell." You could have heard a pin drop and every eye went from Chrissy to Ryan and back again. Holy shit. Things just got more complicated.

"Yes, we do. Sorry, no disrespect intended, but how are you involved in this?"

"I'm an analyst for the FBI, you all knew that. But you didn't know what I analyzed, it's top secret."

Cam wondered if even Meghan knew what Chrissy did for the FBI. Probably not, and now he understood why she hadn't joined Meghan and Miranda on the shopping trip.

"Go ahead, Chrissy," Captain Knox said.

As she set up her computer and started a slideshow of photos from the scene of yesterday's shooting and explained what they were seeing. "I got called into work last night. Originally, my boss thought this was MS-13 activity against the restaurant owner, but then one of the cameras caught part of one of the shooter's faces."

Flipping to the image of the shooter's partial, she then clicked to display the side-by-side with the full image.

Jake spoke first. "He doesn't look familiar."

"No, he wouldn't to you. He's been on our watchlist for quite a while. He was radicalized back in twenty-fourteen. His name is Musafa Arfat."

"So that's what you do? Monitor terrorist threats?" Rafe asked.

"Yes, mostly. Sometimes other stuff too. Depends. I'm good at analyzing scenarios and figuring out puzzles. So I get the nasty, complicated ones."

"Who radicalized him?" Cam asked although he had a feeling he already knew.

"The Taliban, but apparently he and your friend Azfaar have a connection."

"Fuck."

"Exactly," Captain Knox said. "It looks like the Saudi mission was partially wishful thinking and to get you guys out of hiding."

"They were going to try to take us out? He must have his head up his ass," Jake said.

"It looks like it. The intel was accurate about the threat, but you were too quick on following the threads. They were going to try to take out half the team at the bomb site and the other half at the airport. Somehow, they knew our plan. We think the guy Lynch put you in touch with worked for ISIS."

"Azfaar is aligned with ISIS for sure?" Murph asked and then let out a low whistle.

"Yes."

"Why is he all rapid dog on us?" Murph mumbled.

"Because you killed his baby brother. And now he wants revenge," Knox said with a grim expression. "Problem is since he didn't get you on foreign soil our hands are tied. You can't operate her."

"Fuck that," Rafe said. "We're just supposed to sit around and wait for him to pick us off one at a time, or worse our family or women?"

"No, not exactly."

"What does that mean?" Ryan asked. It was the first time he'd spoken since Chrissy had come into the room.

"You all know Tex, right? Ex-SEAL, computer whiz, overall badass? He can pull information from thin air that no one else even knows exists."

They nodded.

"After we got Chrissy's information this morning, I contacted him off the record and had him start digging. We may not be able to operate but we sure as hell can defend ourselves."

It was a modicum of relief, but Cam was itching to go after Miranda and make sure she was safe. He didn't like that she was out there alone with Meghan and they were defenseless.

"Did he find anything?" Cam asked.

"Not yet, but I have no doubt between him and Chrissy we'll find this motherfucker and take out him and anyone else helping him," Jake said.

"Chrissy, you're okay with this? It's not exactly legal?" Ryan asked. Startled, she looked at him. It was the first question directed to her and from the one SEAL who usually ignored her. Cam could just about imagine what he was thinking. They all knew he had it bad for her, but what held him back, they still didn't know.

"I shouldn't be, but you're my friends, and my best friend is a target. So, yeah, I'll deal with the fall out if it comes to that. I was given permission to brief you. Not sure how far that extends, but I'll do what I can."

Ryan nodded. "What's next, Boss? How do you want to handle this?"

"This is where I leave you. As far as Command is concerned, you're all on leave for the next two weeks. I anticipate that this will be handled by then."

Jake nodded, and after the door closed with a loud click, he laid out the part that Chrissy was involved with. It wasn't complicated, and they had to be careful they didn't get in the way of law enforcement. But they were licensed to carry and wouldn't leave the house without a weapon until they'd caught whoever was behind this mess. They had two weeks to get it done.

"Chrissy, you can't tell Meghan and Miranda any of this. At least not yet. We have to be careful of what is shared because it's related to a past mission."

"You're shitting me, right? They're in just as much danger as you guys and you're not going to warn them?"

"We didn't say that. But you can't. Or you'll be laying yourself wide open to a rash of shit. We'll figure out a way to give them enough information to keep them safe."

Chrissy nodded, but she wasn't happy. They weren't even on a mission and were still in the middle of a cluster fuck. How did they keep getting so lucky?

"One other thing, Chrissy. Forget you ever heard Tex's name."

"No problem. I guess I'm dismissed now?"

"Afraid so. You don't need to know the rest of the plan."

After Chrissy left, they mapped out the details. Then they called Tex.

"Tex."

"Hey bro, good to talk to you. You're on

speaker with the team. I know you know Rafe and Cam. But let me introduce you to the team. Ryan McLaughlin and Drew Murphy."

"Too bad we're not meeting under better circumstances."

"No shit," Murph said.

"Have you turned up anything on the guy that Chrissy identified?"

"I haven't located him, but I'm searching social media for any sign of him."

"Hopefully, something turns up soon. From the chatter Chrissy picked up it looks like there is a whole terror cell that we uncovered because they got sloppy."

"Yes, I've been working with the intel that Chrissy shared to try to identify any known associates of Arfat. But they have gotten smarter over the years, and there are so many apps that erase as you go."

"Fucking typical. Let's help the terrorists get more efficient," Murph said.

"It's inevitable, but our technology is better. Don't worry we'll find them. Just think though, if it weren't for Azfaar's vendetta against you, we'd never have found about the cell, or at least not in time to diffuse whatever they're planning."

Tex had a point. It still sucked, but he was right. Cam would have preferred to tackle the asshole on foreign soil, and he knew the team felt the same way. Having to stop the threat this way was much harder and could get them court-martialed if they weren't careful.

"So where does that leave us?" Jake asked.

"I'll keep the trackers active on Meghan and Miranda, but they're only good if they have their phones with them. Other than that, I'll keep digging. As soon as I find anything I'll let you know."

"Copy that. Thanks for always being there for us, Tex. I don't know what we'd all do without you."

"No shit. I'm keeping track of so many of your women now I need a separate computer just for that. Maybe I should start a side hustle."

"You could always put Melody in charge of that part."

"She's got her hands full with the kids, but you never know. Watch your six, and I'll be in touch."

After they disconnected, Jake looked around the table, meeting each one of their eyes. "We're in a shit show here, and I'm not sure how it's going to play out. But if we aren't careful we could all end up off the teams or worse. If you want out of this, say so now."

"What the fuck, Boss? We're a team, brothers, we might as well be the five muskafuckingteers," Murph responded.

They agreed with Murph. No matter what they were in this together.

"Rafe, you and Cam figure out what you're going to tell your women. We don't want to scare them, but they need to take precautions."

They nodded. Cam didn't have a clue what he was going to tell Miranda. The last thing he wanted was to blow a hole in her confidence.

"I think we need to tell them as much as possible. They're smart women, they'll know if we lie to them," Rafe said.

"I agree, but how much can we tell them without sharing top-secret intel?"

After going back and forth, they came up with a basic cover story since the girls knew Azfaar had initially escaped capture. They'd tell them that he hired some people to take out the SEALs as revenge for killing his brother and they needed to be extra vigilant.

CHAPTER 12

THE FOOD AT THE MEXICAN RESTAURANT WAS delicious, and Miranda was stuffed. For a change, it was she and Meghan who'd nearly finished their food. The guys were quiet and hardly ate anything. In fact, if the women hadn't been talking most of the meal it would have been strangely quiet.

She wondered if she'd made Cam mad because she practically insisted they sit outside on the patio so Halo could be with them. But neither she nor Meghan wanted him to be stuck in the car. It wasn't too hot but still, it didn't seem fair. He and Rafe relented but neither looked happy.

"What are you doing tomorrow?" Meghan asked as they paid the check and packed their take-home boxes. "If you don't have plans you could come over and we'll have a big BBQ for the whole team. We haven't done that in a while. What do you think, Rafe?"

"Sounds okay to me. But Cam and Miranda might want some alone time."

Miranda looked at Cam to see if he seemed interested one way or the other, but she couldn't tell. Normally, his face was so animated, but today it was like he was brooding. She wondered what had happened when they were at the base.

"I'll text you later and let you know, okay?" Miranda said.

"No problem. Or we can do it later in the week. It'd just be fun to get together before you go back to Atlanta."

"I agree."

When they reached their trucks, Meghan hugged Miranda and whispered, "if you need to talk I'm just a text or call away. I can come and get you too if there's a problem."

"Thanks, I'm sure it's fine."

"Talk to you later," Rafe said as he helped Meghan into his truck.

When Cam opened the door and let Halo into the back, she'd had enough. "Want to tell me what is going on? You've been weird since we left Target. In fact, your comment about the bathing suit was practically the last thing you've said."

She'd surprised him because it was like he'd

come out of a fog. "I'm sorry. I didn't mean to upset you."

"Is it work? I know you can't talk about it, but you can say yes or no, right?"

"Yes I can say that, and it is kind of about work. Let's just get home and relax and we can talk more."

His reply eased some of the tension that had been building up in her shoulders and stopped her stomach from churning. For a few minutes, she thought she was going to lose her lunch. Then she'd gotten pissed. There was no reason for him to act like this at least not without talking to her about the issue.

"If you don't want to go to Meghan and Rafe's tomorrow that's fine. I came here to spend time with you."

"I know, Sunshine. It's what I want more than anything. I hate that we only have a few days and all of this other stuff is eating into our time. We'll get it figured out."

"As long as you haven't changed your mind about us. If that happens, I'd rather you just tell me than be a jerk about it."

"What? Is that what you think? That I've changed my mind?"

"Maybe. The way you've been acting today is so different, it made me wonder if after last night..."

"No. Just stop. Last night was fucking amazing. Nothing has changed, other than I'm worried about you." By then they'd made it back to his apartment building. After he pulled into a spot, turned off the truck, he turned to look at her. "You are the light in my life, that's not going to change, no matter what. Got it?"

"Got it." She might be the light in his life, but he was definitely her knight in shining armor and Halo was his mini-me. If there hadn't been a console between them, she'd have jumped into his arms and kissed him. But she figured she could wait until they got inside.

Flashing one of his wonderful smiles, he came around to get her and let Halo. She did notice that he took his time looking around before he opened her door. But when he grabbed her hand she forgot all about it. When they got to his apartment, they followed the same routine as the day before.

"Do you do this every time you come home or is it just because I'm here?"

"Every time. It keeps Halo sharp. It's part of his training."

"I hadn't thought of that. I guess he has to train almost as much as the rest of the team." Halo gave them the all clear, and they went into the apartment. In some ways it made her feel safer after Halo checked everything out.

"Sometimes, I think more. He goes in first a lot of the time and makes sure we know what to look for. Like he did when he went into the cave to find you."

"I was never so happy to see anyone when he rubbed his head against my hand, and I saw the American flag on his vest."

"And that's the best part of the job."

"I can imagine that there are lots of times without happy endings."

"It happens, but lots of successes too."

"I'm sorry if I am getting into dangerous territory and asking too many questions."

"You're fine, Sunshine. But we do have something to talk about. But first how about a drink? Water, wine, something else?"

From the dour look on his face, she was thinking she might need something stronger than water. "I'll have a glass of wine."

"Be right back, why don't you pick out a movie."

Cam was going back and forth so much she was starting to wonder if she was losing her mind. She hoped whatever was eating at him, he'd spit it out and they could move on.

~

THE DESIRE TO PUNCH A WALL WAS ALMOST

overwhelming. He was a trained special operator, a frogman, and he fucking knew better. Yet he couldn't control his feelings around Miranda, and it was dangerous. If he wasn't careful, she'd get hurt and it would be his fault.

Ever since Chrissy shared her intel, he'd been going back and forth about what to do. Miranda would be safer if he sent her back home. There was plenty of security there. But she'd never go without a full explanation, and that was something he couldn't give her. The alternative was to break up with her, but then he might as well rip his heart out.

The plan should work but these terror cells were getting more sophisticated all the time. At least with the FBI was in charge of the case they'd get more intel than they would from the police. Chrissy texted him while they were at lunch. When Meghan and Miranda went to the ladies' room, he saw the message. But it didn't uncomplicate anything.

Waiting for Tex to update them was torture, but he needed to focus. It was no different than any other mission, except it was. This time his heart was involved.

Grabbing a bottle of white wine from the fridge and two glasses he went into the living room. Halo was sitting on the couch next to Miranda and getting lots of loving. She was going to spoil that dog rotten by the time she went home.

"Hey, isn't that my spot?"

"You can have this side," she answered and patted the other side of the sofa. Smiling, he sat down and poured their wine.

"Did you pick a movie?"

"Yeah, I figured we might as well stay with the theme. So tonight's feature is Winter Soldier."

"Have you seen it already?"

"Yes, I have, I liked it too. But this way you won't have to feel bad if I fall asleep again. Although, I think I'll be okay today."

"I did have you up most of the night." Her blush never failed to make him smile. The rose color spread across her cheekbones and tinged her whole face until she looked like one of the old fashioned china dolls his sister had when she was a kid.

"That's true. But I'm not complaining."

"I'm happy to hear that. There is something I have to talk to you about before we start the movie."

"Okay…" She was stressed and this time it was entirely his fault.

"I'm sorry if I've been cranky, none of it has to do with you. Like I said downstairs, you are my Sunshine, just like the song says."

"Meghan told me you called me that, but until this visit, I never heard you say it."

"Because we were at your parent's house and it didn't seem right. But after this visit, I doubt I'll be able to hold back next time."

He handed her a wine glass and took a sip of his. Then leaned back against the sofa and pulled her against his side. Cam needed to touch her, to gauge her reaction, her fear when he told her.

"So what's going on, Cam. Like I said before, just rip that Band-Aid off and be done with it."

"Do you remember the man who kept you hostage?"

"Yes," her voice quivered. "I'll never forget. I can see his face as clearly as I see yours."

He hated dredging this up, but they didn't have any other option. "Well even though we killed him we weren't able to capture his brother. He's still out there and he wants revenge."

"Oh my God. Does he blame me? Is he coming for me?"

"No, baby. Not you, he wants the team, and somehow he found out who we are. We think that's who was shooting at us yesterday."

All the color drained out of Miranda's face and the hand that held the wine glass shook so violently he thought she'd either break the stem or dump it all over. Gently, he took and put both glasses on the table. Then he pulled her into his lap and wrapped his arms tightly around her.

"Miranda, look at me." She turned her head and met his eyes. She was still pale as a ghost. "Baby, you are safe. I'm not going to let anything happen to you. I told you because you're here with me. I need you to be vigilant, always aware of your surroundings. If something seems wrong, tell me."

Hoping to quiet her shaking, he rested his lips against her forehead and whispered over and over again that it would be okay. When he didn't get a response, he was worried maybe he needed to call Meghan or her mom, but then she relaxed against him.

"Are you okay, baby?"

"As much as I can be. But you'll keep me safe, right?" And he would. She was his life, and no one was going to take her from him.

"Always, Sunshine. Always."

What she did next managed to surprise him again. She reached for the wine glass, took a large swallow and then turned to him with a big smile on her face. "So how about that movie now. Unless there's more we need to talk about?"

"No, that's everything."

"Good. I think we both deserve some downtime. You start the movie and I'll grab more of that popcorn you bought yesterday." Then she hopped off his lap and headed for the kitchen.

Halo looked just as surprised with the sudden change in mood. Either she was excellent at compartmentalizing or she was in the other room losing it. He'd bet it was the later. But since she wanted privacy, as much as it killed him to do it, he stayed in the living room. Put the movie in and got it set up for when she returned.

If he hadn't looked closely he wouldn't have been able to tell she'd been crying, when she came in with the popcorn. But he didn't say anything, just clicked play and lifted his arm for her to settle against him.

Her breathing calmed as she leaned against him and he hoped she'd be able to relax and enjoy the movie. If not, he had another way to make sure she'd be relaxed and happy and entirely worn out afterward. In fact, he'd prefer that option to the movie anyway.

CHAPTER 13

Miranda focused on Cam's breathing in an effort to steady hers. She'd freaked out, scared herself, and worried him. There was danger but it wasn't aimed at her based on what Cam told her. There was no reason for him to lie to her. So why had she lost it?

PTSD. She answered her own question. Everyone around her saw it, and she'd tried to ignore it. Put it up on a shelf in a pretty jar that could be left to get dusty. Except it refused to be ignored. The movie and wine would help, so would snuggling with Cam, but it wouldn't make it go away. Or prevent the inevitable nightmare that would visit her later. It was time for her to take control. Cam was right, seeing a therapist would rehash everything, but it would get it out in the open and help her work through her fear.

"More wine, Sunshine?" Cam's voice was filled with concern. No wonder he'd been moody, he'd been worried about her reaction on top of not knowing where the threat would come from next.

"Yes, please."

"I still can't believe Robert Redford is an actual octopus?"

"I know."

"Do you want to watch something else? It's obvious you're not paying attention."

"What?"

"You just agreed that Robert Redford is a real octopus."

"Dang, sorry. I do want to see this. I was just thinking."

"Do you want to talk about it?"

"Not yet. I'm fine, really, and we will. But right now, I want to snuggle and watch the movie."

"You got it, nothing I enjoy more, okay, maybe there's one thing," he answered and lifted her chin for a quick kiss.

"I hope that option isn't off the table?"

"Are you kidding me? It's always on the table and can literally be if you want to give it a try." He waggled his eyebrows and it cracked her up. They moved so much it was hysterical. The laughter helped her unwind a bit. The wine did the rest.

Sharing the remainder of the bottle of wine and the bowl of popcorn, then watched the movie. As the afternoon wore on, Miranda relaxed, the threats pushed back into the recess of her mind, for now.

"I never get tired of that movie. But damn what Hydra did to Bucky, fuck."

"He was a jerk at the end of the other movie. Jealous of Cap. But you're right, no one deserves to go through what they did to him."

"What do you want to do now? Watch another movie? Grab an early dinner? Go out for a drink? Stay in for more drinks?"

"Wow so many options. What to do, what to do?" She tapped her finger against her lips and batted her eyelashes. The wine and the movie had helped her relax. But the thought of going out set her heart racing. "I have an idea. Since we were in 'Mexico' for lunch how about 'China' or 'Japan' for dinner? Someone must deliver, right?"

"Yeah, or I can go and pick it up."

"Delivery is better. We've had a few glasses of wine, it's safer to not drive." She doubted that she fooled him, but he didn't disagree.

"That's true. I have some menus, let's see which country appeals to you more based on food choices." She was relieved he played along. They could have a picnic in the living room and watch another movie.

After much back and forth, they decided on Chinese and Cam called in the order. "It'll be here in twenty minutes."

"That's so funny."

"What is?"

"It's just I can't remember a time when I ordered Chinese food and they didn't say twenty minutes, can you? It's like their standard response."

Cam laughed. "You're right, they always say it. Sometimes they get here faster sometimes longer, but you're right. They always say twenty. I wonder if it's on a post-it next to all phones in Chinese restaurants."

"You know, we're going to have to experiment. Every time we order, let's order from a different restaurant and see what they say, just to prove our hypothesis."

"Are you going to want that much Chinese food while you're here?"

"I didn't mean all on this trip. We can order from my house too, and when I'm back. And I've been meaning to talk to you about something."

"You have?"

"Don't freak out. It's nothing bad. Well, I don't think it is. Not sure how you'll feel about it."

"Dammit, woman. Spit it out already. For fuck's sake. Now I know how you were feeling."

"It sucks doesn't it," she said with a smile. She

hadn't meant to torture him, but it was a little payback for earlier. "I think I'm going to move here if I can find a job." Silence. His face was unreadable. Maybe he didn't want her around all the time. It's not like she said she was going to move in with him. Just to the same state.

"Or not. I thought it would be nice to see you more often. Chrissy offered to let me stay with her while I look for a job and apartment."

"It's wonderful. But why stay with Chrissy or look for an apartment? Don't you want to move in with me?"

"I didn't want to push myself on you. We haven't been around each other all that much, and I didn't want you to feel obligated. I'm not sure you're even happy about the idea of me moving here."

"Of course I'm happy, thrilled. Ecstatic, even." Then he scooped her off the couch and swung her around. Halo started jumping up and down and barking. He proved his point and made her dizzy. If he didn't stop soon he was going to be wearing the wine and popcorn she'd eaten. Thankfully, the buzzer rang, and she was saved.

Cam put her down then stopped by the front door and took a gun from the table drawer. After looking through the peephole, he tucked it into the back of his waistband and grabbed his wallet. Seeing the gun surprised her and reminded her of what he'd said about being vigilant. She needed to calm down before she gave herself a heart attack. A nice headline that would be, 'Senator's daughter scares herself to death, news at eleven.' Yeah her father would be thrilled, and her mother would drag her back to life just so she could give her hell.

After he closed and locked the door, he slipped the gun back into the drawer and carried the bag over to the coffee table. "Did you want to eat in here and watch another movie?"

"Yes, it'll be like a picnic."

"How do you like to eat yours? Chopsticks, fork, on a plate, or from the container."

"I'd love to eat it from the container with chopsticks. I've always wanted to do that after seeing them do it in movies."

"Chopsticks it is then," he said with a smile. "Anything for my Sunshine." They pushed the table farther from the couch and sat on the floor. Cam unpacked the food and then got some napkins and another bottle of wine from the kitchen."

"Do you always keep this much wine around?

"No, not so much. I don't drink that much when I'm home. But it's usually beer if I do. But I knew you liked wine and I bought a few bottles yesterday."

"I can tell. We can drink beer if you want. It goes good with this food."

"Nah, we started with wine and I am enjoying it."

The food smelled delicious and they'd ordered way more than they could eat. Until she remembered how little Cam had eaten at lunch and changed her mind about how much would be left. As much as she wanted to dig in, she thought they should finish their conversation.

Cam grabbed a pot sticker and was about to pop it into his mouth when he looked at her. "Something wrong?"

"No, it looks great, but I wondered if we should finish our conversation first."

"Oh. We can but how about we eat and talk because I'm starving." The look on his face reminded her of a little boy, and she couldn't refuse him. She was hungry too which surprised her since she'd stuffed herself at lunch.

"Okay. I don't want to keep food from a growing boy." Grabbing a set of chopsticks, she opened the container of General Tso's chicken. It was perfect, crispy with just the right amount of heat and sweetness. "This is so good."

"Yeah? I haven't tried it yet." Before she realized what he was doing, he'd reached into the box with his chopsticks and grabbed a piece. Then he popped it into his mouth. "Mmmm, you're right, it's fucking wonderful."

"Hey, that's my food. Hands off."

"Sorry." He tried to look contrite, but he didn't come close to pulling it off.

"No, you're not. But I'm watching you. Try it again and I'll bite your fingers."

"You'd deny a starving SEAL a bit of food."

"Yes, because there's a ton of other food on this table, Mr. Badass."

"Mr. Badass, huh?" Before she realized, he'd put down his food and tackled her onto the floor, leaning over her and laughing. "I'll show you badass."

"Holy crap you can move fast," she said between giggles.

"You ain't seen nothing, sweetheart," Cam said in a Humphrey Bogart impersonation. It was terrible and made her laugh even harder.

"I haven't?"

"Not even a little bit." Then he leaned down and molded his lips against hers, their passion igniting like wildfire. When he released her, they were out of breath. "That was just a taste, later you'll be getting the whole lesson."

The pure desire in his voice, heated her to her core and her hunger wasn't for the food now she wanted the man.

~

After helping her sit back up, he handed

her a fresh pair of chopsticks since hers had been tossed when he tackled her. Was he sorry? Not even a little bit. The woman took his breath away. She'd surprised him when she brought up moving. He'd been wondering how to broach the subject. He'd come up with the idea while he was bored in Afghanistan.

Atlanta was just a few hours away by plane, but it might as well have been California. It was hard for him to get away for days at a time, his schedule was frenetic and fluid, and he couldn't put in for time off whenever he wanted to see her. He needed her in his life. Why wouldn't she think he wanted her to move in? He thought he'd made it clear that he wanted her. Maybe he needed to lay it out there. The only thing holding him back was worry that it would scare her away. She led such a different life, and her parents were more uptight than the colonel and that was saying something.

"Miranda, nothing would make me happier than for you to move in here. I've been trying to figure out how to bring it up for the last few weeks."

"While you were away?"

"Yes. You're too far away in Atlanta. But I know your roots are there, your friends, and family. I wasn't sure how you'd feel. Or if it was too soon to bring it up."

"I was worried that coming here would make you feel boxed in. We haven't talked about our relationship, or where it could go. I didn't know if this was a casual thing for you. I didn't want you to feel forced into a relationship you weren't looking to have."

"Never, Sunshine. I thought I'd made it clear how much I wanted you."

"Wanted, yes you did. But wanting doesn't mean a relationship. It could have been just about the sex."

"No. It was never about that. From the first moment, I saw you in that cave you had me. I wasn't lying when I told you that. You were so brave even though you'd been through hell."

"That's not special."

"Yes, it is. I've been part of many rescues and most women who'd been through what you had would have been basket cases, broken, sometimes they won't even let us touch them. So yes, you are very special."

As he watched her take in his words, every emotion played across her face. There was no way he'd ever let her play poker. She couldn't hide anything.

"Okay, then. Looks like we might have some plans to make before I go back."

"Hell yeah." Leaning over, he kissed her. "We should celebrate."

"We are, Chinese picnic and wine."

"I have something a little different in mind."

"But I'm hungry, and you're eating all the food," she said with a smile. When he looked at the table, he realized she was right. He had eaten most of the food.

"Damn, I'm so sorry. I guess I was hungrier than I thought."

Laughing, she held up her box of General Tso's. She'd been clutching it like a favorite doll. "You didn't get everything, though. I still have this and no, you're not getting anymore."

"No problem," Cam said as he popped the last pot sticker into his mouth. Then searched in the bag for the fortune cookies. Cracking one open, he pulled out his fortune.

"What does it say," she asked as she picked up another piece of chicken.

Cam read it twice before he read the words out loud, "Your life will be filled with sunshine."

CHAPTER 14

"Let me see, that can't be real," Miranda demanded as she held out her hand. He had to be making that up.

"I swear, it is. Look." He dropped the little white slip of paper into her palm and sure enough, that is exactly what it said.

"That's kind of freaky."

"I don't think so. It's my fortune, and for a change, I'd say they nailed it. This is one I'm going to hold on to. Just have to figure out a way to frame it."

"We'll figure something out. It's just so bizarre. Wait till I tell Meghan, she's not going to believe it either."

"She might. Stranger things have happened for all of us. Look how she and Rafe met."

"I don't know their story."

"Oh, I thought she might have told you. They met while stuck in Norfolk Airport. Their plane was delayed for something like twelve hours. If that's not fate, I don't know what is. He was with her when she found out about the abduction. It was on TV."

"Wow. That sure seems like fate. I can't imagine how she felt when she found out, especially that way."

"Me either. Rafe put her in touch with a friend of ours to try to help her find out more information. We weren't involved until we got sent for you."

"I guess I can thank my dad for that."

"Yes, but it's what we do."

"You were supposed to save the others from the group too, right?"

"You know I can't talk about my missions, except the one you were there for."

"Sorry." He was hiding something. The way he answered that question was odd. The rest of the missionary group was rescued after they found her. Didn't that mean it was the same mission?

"No worries. There is one other thing I need to tell you. I should have told you before."

"What is it? Do we have to have the Band-Aid talk again?"

"No," Cam said and grinned. He might be

smiling now, but she'd bet anything that they'd be talking about those sticky things way too much.

"So…spit it out then."

"The friend Rafe told Meghan about? His name is Tex. He's an ex-SEAL, lost his leg on a mission. But he's a computer genius."

While he spoke, she continued eating the spicy chicken. It was weird he was stalling.

"Anyway, I put a tracker on your phone when I visited you in Atlanta."

"You're spying on me?"

"No, and I figured that's what you'd think. It was only that if something happened so we could find you. It's for your protection. We have Meghan's phone tracked too."

"Does she know?"

"Yeah, Rafe told her a while ago." Miranda wasn't sure if she was upset or not about being tracked. It was understandable after everything, but why not just tell her?

"And you didn't want to tell me?"

"I was going to, but I didn't want you worrying you were still in danger." She would have too. Even without knowing, she worried.

"Okay."

"Okay? You're not mad?"

"Nope. It makes sense, and you're right. I would have worried. When will you stop?"

"I don't know. I'd prefer not to. It took the

edge off knowing Tex could locate you if something happened, especially while I was on a mission."

"I guess it's okay for now. I'd like to meet or at least talk to him though. It's weird he knows what I'm doing. I'm sure my dad would have a fit."

"Oh yeah, no doubts there. But you don't have to tell him either. We'll call Tex tomorrow so you can talk to him. And he doesn't constantly watch you. But if something happened, he could find you as long as you have your phone with you."

"No cameras though, right? He's not a peeping Tex is he?"

Cam chuckled. She loved that sound. "No peeping Tex, but I'm going to have to tell him that. He'll get a kick out of it and so will his wife, Melody."

"Can I ask you something?"

"Always, as long as it's not about work, I don't have any secrets anymore."

"Why tell me now? Is there more going on than what you said earlier?"

"No. But because of that, I thought it might reassure you. That you're really safe."

As she dug around inside the cardboard box for just the right piece of chicken, she considered his words. Did it make her feel safer or just spied on? She wasn't sure yet, but if the Tex person wasn't actually watching her, it didn't feel as creepy.

"I'm not sure if it does or not. I'll let you know. But I'm not mad if that's what you're worried about."

"Tex is one of the good guys. I promise."

"If you trust him, then I suppose I need to trust him too. Now, did you save me a fortune cookie, or did you eat them all?"

"Here you go."

"Thanks. I wonder what visionary words I will find." Her phone rang with a familiar tone before she had a chance to tear open the plastic wrapper.

"Hi, Mom." Cam grinned and then picked up the empty containers and took them in the kitchen.

"You didn't call me back."

"We were busy running around today. And just finished dinner."

"Is everything okay there? Is he treating you well?"

"Mom, I'm not fifteen on my first date with Thad."

"Of course you're not. But it doesn't mean I can't worry." She loved her mom. She truly did but sometimes the woman drove her crazy.

"I'm safe here, I am surrounded by Navy SEALs. I doubt I'd be safer in the White House."

"I don't know about that," Cherise Stanhope said.

"How are things there? Is Dad home?"

"Yes, he got in this morning and he's staying for the weekend. He was sorry he missed you."

"Tell him I said hi. I love you. I'll talk to you tomorrow. Okay?" Her mother's sigh was loud and clear over the phone, but if Miranda didn't cut her off now, she'd talk to her for at least an hour, extracting every detail of her day and then some.

"I love you too. Goodbye."

"That was pretty quick," Cam said as he came back in from the kitchen with Halo at his heels.

"Did you feed him? He's licking his chops."

"Yup. I think he was disappointed I didn't have any leftovers and he had to eat his food."

"I bet. I'd be too after smelling the Chinese food."

"I need to take him for a walk. I don't want to leave you alone, so you get to come too."

"A walk sounds wonderful."

~

WHILE MIRANDA WAS TALKING TO HER MOTHER, Cam checked in with Jake. They hadn't heard anything from Tex yet, which wasn't a good sign. He'd hoped that he'd have identified the other shooter or at least some known associates by now. Grabbing the gun from the drawer he tucked it in his waist and pulled his shirt down to keep it hidden before going back into the living room. With any luck, Miranda wouldn't notice.

After he finished clearing away dinner and putting her leftovers in the refrigerator, they took Halo out for a walk.

"I can't believe he hasn't had to go all afternoon."

"He's a good dog and soldier."

"That's for sure," she said as they walked to the crosswalk. Cam checked their surroundings before crossing the street. Halo was calm and hadn't detected any threats either.

"Do you think we can go to the beach tomorrow? Or will you have to go to work again?"

"The beach sounds great. Are you going to wear your new suit? It looked fantastic."

"Maybe. Probably."

"No pressure, Sunshine. But you looked amazing."

"Thank you, but I think you might be a wee bit prejudiced."

"I don't think so. Meghan said the same thing."

"How about we change the subject?" She was adorable and totally oblivious to her beauty. He was so used to dating women who thought they were all that and a bag of chips. Meeting her and Meghan had been a real eye-opener. It was no wonder he didn't want to let Miranda out of his sight.

"What would you like to talk about?"

"Tell me more about your family. Other than your sister, you haven't mentioned them. I don't even know where you grew up."

"My dad was in the Navy too, did his twenty-five years and retired. I grew up in Virginia Beach, so this is home for me. My sister lives in New York now, but my parents are still here."

"Do you see them a lot?"

"Not as much as I should. But I talk to them at least once a week when I'm home. And we always spend the holidays together as long as I'm not on a mission."

"Will I get to meet them?"

"Of course. I didn't think we'd have time this trip, but since you're going to move here..." He left it hanging because they'd never finished that discussion. "You are going to move in with me right?"

"Are you asking?"

"Fuck yeah, I am. I'll beg if I have to." Miranda giggled and looked like she was considering it. "Wait, you're not going to make me beg, are you?"

Before she had a chance to answer, Halo

growled. "What is it?" Cam asked the dog. Glancing around, he didn't see anything, but Halo had. He noticed movement in the trees across the parking lot just before the first shot rang out, followed by four more. It wasn't the same as the machine gun drive-by, but he didn't doubt it was the same crew.

"Get down, now," Cam yelled, as he pushed Miranda down to the ground. Then he let Halo off his leash. "Go get him." The desire to chase the shooter warred with the need to keep her safe and her safety won out. With his gun in one hand and his phone in the other, he dialed Jake.

"Under fire near the apartment." Then he disconnected the call and called nine-one-one. For the second time in two days, he'd had to shield her from gunfire, and he was furious.

"Are you okay?"

"I'm fine. Just a little freaked out. When is this going to stop?"

"Soon, Sunshine, soon. I promise. One way or another," he answered as he helped her to her feet. He'd rather get her inside, but they needed to wait for the police.

Halo returned with a piece of cloth in his mouth, and Cam shoved it into his pocket. Jake and Ryan arrived a few minutes later.

"That was quick."

"We were at The Ready Room having a beer,"

Jake answered. "Are you okay?" The question was directed at Miranda, not him, and she nodded.

"Halo came back with this. Looks like traces of blood," Cam said as he handed it to Jake.

"Shouldn't you give that to the police," Miranda asked.

"We'll be able to identify the guy faster if we keep it."

"You mean that Tex person?" Jake looked at Cam and he shrugged.

"No, Chrissy."

"Chrissy is involved?"

"Not officially. But she has the access and can get this identified faster than if we go through the police. Plus they won't share their info with us."

"And you don't trust the police to catch these people?"

"It's not that, we're just better at it. It's what we do."

"But you don't do it here. So basically, I'm not supposed to know this."

Cam grinned. She was a smart woman. But he'd known that already. "It would help if you didn't."

"I know nothing then."

"Good, girl."

The police arrived a few minutes later. One of the first things Cam said was he had a gun, and then put it down on the ground. The last thing he wanted was a jumpy cop thinking he was a threat.

Jake and Ryan waited in Jake's truck while the police questioned them. This was becoming a habit. It would be bad enough if it was just him, but Miranda was in danger just from being around him.

The crime scene techs showed up and Cam led them over to where he thought the shooter was standing. There was no sign of him but there was blood on the ground. Under his breath, he whispered good boy. Halo might not have taken him down, but he definitely got a piece of him.

"You said you sent the dog after him?"

"Yes, he's trained just like your K-9 officers."

"Looks like he found him. Did he bring back any evidence?"

Cam wasn't used to lying to anyone, let alone the police, but this time it was necessary. "Nope, nothing. Think you'll be able to ID him from the blood?"

"We'll see. Maybe we'll be lucky and there will be prints on these casings. Any idea why he shot at you?"

"No, I don't. We were walking the dog."

"And the other day, you were involved in the drive-by, weren't you?"

"Yeah. We were there."

"Too much of a coincidence. I don't like coincidences." This guy was definitely more experienced than the one who'd been at the last scene. He was suspicious too. Not that Cam blamed him, he'd be in his shoes.

"I'm not very fond of them myself," Cam answered. Miranda had stayed across the street and was giving her statement to another officer. He'd left Halo with her as protection. Not that he didn't trust the cops, but the dog has faster reflexes. "Are we done, or do you have more questions for me."

"We're done for now. I have your contact information if I need to follow up. But most likely it will be Detective Black."

"I'll be around. We're on leave."

"I'll make a note of that. And the Senator's daughter?"

"She'll be here for a few more days. Then she'll be going back to Atlanta next Monday." The cop nodded and made a few more notes as they headed over to where Miranda was with the other officer.

"Everything okay," Cam asked as he took Miranda's hand.

"Yes, fine. I think we're all done."

"Yes, ma'am. We'll be in touch if we have any further questions." Then they walked over to where the crime scene techs were working.

"Are you okay?" Cam asked and hugged her.

"Yes, I guess I'm getting used to being shot at. I'm not nearly as freaked out today."

"I don't think that's a good thing."

"No, it's not. But it's better than a total meltdown."

"That's true. Halo, you're a good boy." Cam rubbed the dog behind the hears. He'd gotten them their best clue unless Tex could pull up something on a traffic cam or some other camera in the area.

"You want to grab a drink and we can talk about this?" Jake asked as he and Ryan came up to them.

"You up for going out, Miranda. Or would you rather go back to the apartment?"

"Can Halo come?"

"Of course, it's The Ready Room, they love him there."

"Then, yes, let's go. I could use a shot of whiskey."

CHAPTER 15

IT WAS WHERE THEY SPENT MOST OF THEIR TIME together. The Ready Room was the place to be if you were a SEAL. The place was packed and with a lot of other SEAL teams. True to Cam's word, Halo was welcome in the bar and walked in like he owned the place. Miranda hadn't been in many bars in her life, so she hadn't known what to expect. This one was filled with pictures and just about anything you could associate with the Navy. It was like walking into another world.

Murph, Rafe, and Meghan were sitting at a table in the back of the bar. From the amount of beer left in the pitcher, they'd been there for a while.

"I didn't think everyone would be here."

"When I called Jake, he called the others."

"Miranda, are you okay? I can't believe this keeps happening," Meghan asked as she jumped up to hug her.

"I'm fine. Cam is great at pushing me out of danger."

"He'd better be," Murph said, "it's what we're trained to do, among other things." Then he waggled his eyebrows. There was no doubt that he was the black sheep of their 'family.'

"Enough," Jake said as he sat down at the table. It was like he'd flipped a switch, and for the first time since Afghanistan, Miranda saw the team mission ready. "I called Chrissy while we were waiting for the cops to finish up. She'll be here in a few minutes."

"What does Chrissy have to do with this," Meghan asked. That surprised, Miranda. She'd figured she was the only one in the dark.

"I'll leave it up to her as to what she wants to tell you, but since it's job-related, probably not much," Jake answered. Meghan looked surprised but just nodded.

A waitress came over with another pitcher of beer and more mugs. Her nametag said Pam and from the way she joked around with the guys, she knew them well.

"Is everyone good, or can I bring something else?"

Cam squeezed her hand to get her attention. "Did you still want a whiskey?"

"Yes, I do," she answered and looked up at Pam. "Do you have Macallan?"

"Yes we do, the twelve single or double cask?"

"Oooh, double please."

"Anyone need anything else?" Pam asked and then went to get Miranda's scotch.

"I didn't take you for a scotch drinker."

"My dad is, and I picked it up from him. But most of the time I just drink wine."

"That would explain it, and he's got good taste too."

"My mother wouldn't have it any other way," she said with a laugh. Miranda figured they were stalling until Pam came back with her drink and Chrissy got there.

Pam was back with her scotch faster than she'd expected. "Look who I found at the front." And there was Chrissy. Miranda was anxious to hear what was going on, but she wasn't sure how much they'd share.

"Do you want anything, Chrissy?"

"Beer is fine, thanks, Pam."

"Okay, signal if you need anything."

Rafe pulled over a chair for Chrissy from the next table and put it between Meghan and Jake. Sitting down, she picked up a mug and took a swallow.

"Thanks for coming, Chrissy. I know you were going to try to stay in the background, but we need your help."

"No problem. If I get fired I can always see about a job with the CIA." Miranda wasn't sure if she was joking or not but hoped she was.

"It shouldn't come to that, but if it does, I'm sure the captain will put in a good word for you."

"Thanks. So where's this evidence you have?" Jake pulled the piece of fabric that Halo had ripped from the shooter and handed it to Chrissy. She put it in an evidence bag, marked and sealed it.

"The police found blood at the scene, so they'll be running it too, but they don't know we have this. Figured your lab would be quicker."

"Has Tex found out anything else?" It looked like everyone knew about this Tex guy but her.

"Not that he's told us. But he had to cast a pretty wide net," Jake answered.

"I realize we have to wait for information, but I'm getting tired of being shot at. And how come we're the ones being targeted?" Cam asked.

Miranda had wondered that herself. It did seem weird that if they were targeting the team that they'd been the only ones dodging bullets.

"Good question. Maybe it isn't the team after all?"

Oh great, just what she'd needed to hear. "So it's me they're trying to kill? What did I do to them?"

"Let's not jump to conclusions. We've been keeping out of sight since this happened. You were an easy target when you were out with Halo."

It was a plausible explanation. But were they just trying to make her feel better?

"What's the plan, Boss?" Ryan asked the question they were all wondering.

"We'll give Chrissy time to ID the shooter from today and Tex time to finish his deep dive into wherever he looks. If we can figure out who we're dealing with, it will make it easier. If not, we'll bait them."

The men nodded in unison, but the women exchanged looks and Miranda was sure they were thinking the same thing she was, that it sounded too dangerous.

"I don't like waiting around," Murph complained.

"None of us do, but we have to give Tex and Chrissy time to see what they can find out. The more we know the better. How many times have we bitched about the lack of intel?"

"Too fucking many," Rafe answered. Re-thinking the whole scotch ideas as her stomach churned, she wondered what that meant for their missions. Losing Cam wasn't an option she wanted to think about, even though she knew it was a real possibility. But if someone in the government screwed up and she found out about it, they'd be sorry.

"Everyone good?"

"I don't like this at all," Meghan said.

Rafe looked surprised and covered the hand she had resting on her mug. "It'll be okay. It sounds much worse than it is."

"It sounds like a fucked up plan to me. Using anyone as bait is not acceptable."

"If that's what it takes to make sure no one is hurt, then that's what we do," Jake answered. "It's what we always do—whatever it takes to get the mission done."

"But this isn't one of your missions. Can't you just let the police do their job?"

"Sure we could do that, but I don't want to sit in the house and worry about you every time you step out the door," Rafe said. "It's just too dangerous to wait. Not when we have other options."

The air deflated from Meghan's argument when he made it about her, and Miranda couldn't fault her for it either. What could they say? Chrissy had been quiet, and Miranda wondered what she was thinking, and which side of the argument she agreed with.

"Are we good now? Anything else that needs to be discussed?" Jake asked as he looked around the table.

"What about Chrissy's phone?" Ryan asked.

"What about my phone?"

"Right, thanks for the reminder. If you're okay with it, I'd like to put a tracker on your phone."

"What the fuck for? Why would you need to track me?"

"It's more of a precaution. We have them in Meghan and Miranda's phones too."

Meghan nodded. "Tex sent me one when I went to Afghanistan and thank God too. Or Rafe never would have found me."

"Okay I get that, but why do you need it now?"

"It's a precaution. If something goes sideways, Tex can locate you. I promise we're not stalking you."

Chrissy sighed. It was apparent she didn't like the idea, but it wasn't necessarily a bad one. "Do you have them too?"

Jake looked surprised at the question. "No, of course not. We're special operators that's a big fuck no."

"It's a double standard then?" Miranda asked.

"Couldn't something happen to you just as easily?"

"But we're together most of the time and there are safeguards built in."

"Fine," Chrissy said as she handed Jake her phone. "But after this shit is done, it's coming out. If I want to run naked through the streets of Williamsburg it's none of your fucking business."

"Well fuck, if you're going to do that, can you call me first? I want to watch," Murph said.

"If I wanted you to know, I'd leave the fucking tracker in." Ryan looked relieved at Chrissy's answer and Miranda hid her smile. How could she not see that Ryan was interested in her?

"I'll let you know if I hear anything from Tex."

"And I'll let Jake know when the results come back. It's the weekend so I'm not sure how fast it will be," Chrissy said as she got up from the table. "I'm out of here." Then she whispered something to Meghan as she passed her on the way out.

"Who's going to take us back to the apartment. We seem to always be without transportation."

"We'll take you."

"Or we can, we bought you here," Jake answered. Miranda hoped he'd pick Rafe so she could talk to Meghan and find out what Chrissy said.

"Thanks, Jake, but I think we'll go with Rafe. It looks like the women want to talk." She could have kissed him for reading her thoughts, but she'd save it for later when they were alone.

~

THIS HAD BECOME A COLOSSAL SHIT SHOW AND Cam didn't like it. Yes, Jake was right, and they needed to give Tex a chance to dig up the information, or at least find a link back to Azfaar. If that didn't happen, it wouldn't matter how many of them they took out, they'd just keep coming.

The women whispered to each other during the short ride from the bar to the apartment building. When they pulled up in front of the building, he, Halo, and Rafe checked for threats before he helped Miranda from the back seat.

"Thanks for the ride."

"Call me later," Meghan said as she hugged Miranda then hopped into the passenger seat.

Halo led the way into the building as usual, always on alert. Cam couldn't have asked for a better partner to help keep Miranda safe, even though they hadn't been doing such a great job.

Back in the apartment, he braced himself for a battery of questions, but none came. Instead, Miranda went into the kitchen and made a pot of coffee.

"Won't it keep you up all night?"

"Huh?"

"The coffee. Can you sleep after drinking this late? It's after eight."

"It won't bother me. I think I'm immune to it."

"I'm gonna grab a shower, be right back."

"Okay," she said but sounded distracted. What was she thinking about, or maybe what was she planning would be the better question?

Cam had just finished soaping up when the bathroom door opened. Normally, he'd have pulled back the curtain and reached for the gun, but he knew who it was. "Miranda? Everything okay?"

"It might have been Halo."

"Last I checked he didn't have opposable thumbs and can't use a doorknob."

"True," she answered as she pulled back the curtain. "Mind if I join you?" That she needed to ask when all she had to do was look down at his hard-on, amazed him. He'd reacted instantly to the sight of her naked body in the steamy mist like some kind of forest nymph.

"Are you kidding? Anytime, fuck, every time." She giggled. It was a perfect mixture of sweet and sexy, and it drove him crazy.

Not bothering to rinse the soap off, he pulled the shower head down and held it over her.

Watching her move under the water was extremely erotic. He couldn't wait to get his hands on her. Putting the shower head back, he grabbed the shampoo.

"Do you mind?"

"Not at all," her voice was deeper, huskier and caused his throbbing dick to twitch even more. She was going to be the death of him.

Pouring shampoo onto her head, he massaged it into her hair until it was a mass of suds.

"I think you'd better let me rinse that out or we'll be here for hours."

"Would that be so bad?"

"No, as long as the hot water lasts." Cam chuckled, he planned to have her so distracted she wouldn't notice the water temperature. After she rinsed her hair, he grabbed the soap and got to touch her body at last.

Rubbing the bar between his hands, he started at her neck and worked his way down, until he'd covered every inch of her in soap. Then grabbed the shower head, and rinsed her off, following the same path.

"Spread your legs a little more, baby," Cam asked as he twisted the shower head to give him a more focused spray. He knelt down and held rinsed her folds, working the spray up and down until she was soap free. Then he directed the spray on her clit, moving the shower head in circles as he slid two fingers into her core.

"Oh God. What..."

"Don't you just love adjustable shower heads."

"Mmm."

"Sunshine, lean against the wall, I don't want you to slip." She didn't answer him but did as he suggested. Her quivering increased and her muscles grasped and clenched his fingers. Watching her expression as she got closer to her orgasm, was a huge turn on. Her muscled grew taught and her skin flushed a deep pink. It was incredibly sexy. He wanted to draw it out, give her as much pleasure as he could, but he couldn't refrain tasting her. Almost as soon as he touched her clit, she came, her juices pouring over his fingers and mixing with the water.

"Oh my God. I can barely stand."

"Hold on, let me rinse off and you won't have to."

Making quick work of it, he turned the water off and wrapped her in a towel. Then he carried her to the bedroom and put her on the bed. He should dry off, but his cock was about to explode.

Sliding his wet body over hers, he pushed her thighs apart with his leg. "You are fucking amazing."

As she reached for him, he slid his throbbing shaft deep into her soaking wet core. Even after all the sex the night before, she was still so damn tight. Hot, wet, tight, it just didn't get any better.

Grabbing him around the neck and pulling him to her, she kissed him, biting his lips and then sucking his tongue into her mouth. When she bit down on his tongue, it was like a jolt of electricity traveled straight to his cock. Thrusting into her harder and faster, his balls slapped against her ass. When he couldn't hold back any longer he exploded inside her.

Breathless, he pulled her with him so she could rest on top of him as he rolled onto his back. It was freakin' amazing, but like last night, he was still hard. He hadn't been able to stay hard after an orgasm since he was in his early twenties.

Looking down on his Sunshine, she hadn't moved. Her hair was spread across his chest as her cheek was over his heart. He wished they could stay like that forever.

"That was incredible," she whispered.

"It's you, Sunshine. You have stolen my heart. You're so brave, sexy, funny, and just fucking amazing. You take my breath away. I love you." He hadn't intended for it to pop out like that, but every word was true, and he wasn't sorry. He wasn't sure how she would react, but he didn't have to wait long for his answer.

When she lifted her head to look at him, a huge bright smile lit her face making her glow bright as the sun. "I love you, Cam. You take my breath away too." Then she moved up his body, leaned over his face until her hair covered them like a curtain and kissed him.

"You're mine now, forever and always," he said against her lips.

"And you're mine."

CHAPTER 16

THEY NEEDED ANOTHER SHOWER WHEN THEY got out of bed a few hours later. If this was making love with the man of your dreams, Miranda never wanted it to stop. Sex had never come close to the mind-blowing experience she'd had with Cam. And he promised it was just the beginning. She wondered if she'd be able to walk in the morning.

This time she jumped into the shower alone. Halo needed a walk, but Cam promised he'd stay near the front of the building and would be back before she finished her shower. He still made her promise not to leave the apartment for any reason. He had to be crazy if he thought she had the energy for anything other than the shower. Her legs felt like rubber and she was a bit sore, but she'd do it again in a heartbeat, as long as she didn't have to stand up.

Giggling, she dragged the comb through her hair, which had turned into a ton of knots. Even washing and conditioning it again didn't help much. Maybe she should go shorter, like Meghan. It was an idea and would be easier to care for. Turning on the blow dryer, she never heard the gunshot that blew out the lock on the door, and it wasn't until the bathroom door was thrown open that she realized she was in trouble.

It was like a scene from a movie playing out in her head. A woman is naked in the bathroom when a maniacal killer breaks into her house and stabs her a million times. Except it wasn't a movie, and it wasn't a knife he was pointing at her it was a semi-automatic gun.

"You're coming with me."

"No."

"Alive or dead, you're coming. Your choice," he said in heavily accented English. Miranda couldn't tell if it was Pashto like her abductors in Afghanistan or something different. Either way, she couldn't speak more than a few words of Pashto so it wouldn't help much.

If he'd gotten into the apartment, where were Cam and Halo? Had they ambushed them outside? Killed them and then come for her? She prayed that he was still alive to come for her because she'd rather die than be a captive again. Then she remembered the tracker in her phone and had to figure out a way to bring it with her.

"I'll come. But I need to put clothes on." She'd almost forgotten she was naked with just the brush and a hairdryer for protection. Not helpful unless he was standing in a puddle of water.

Dressed in a traditional Al-Qaeda headdress, his face was mostly covered, and all she could see were his cold dark eyes. As those cruel eyes slowly traveled down her naked body, she doubted he'd let her get dressed. But she refused to move or show weakness. Instead, she gritted her teeth and wished for a miracle.

Finally, he nodded. "Go. Be quick." The asshat didn't even move out of the doorway and forced her to slide past him to get to the bedroom. When she'd joined Cam in the shower earlier she'd just tossed her clothes on the side of the bed, they were still there and so was her phone. Thank God she'd put it in her pocket when they walked Halo earlier. She looked up at the ceiling and said a little thank you. She'd been given her miracle.

Quickly getting dressed she slid the phone underneath her breast inside her bra, it seemed to be the best chance of her captors not finding it. If he'd followed her into the bedroom she'd never have gotten away with it, but she heard him talking and by the time he came into the doorway she was dressed.

Stepping into the room, he grabbed her and dragged her toward the door. It brought back all the horrors of Afghanistan and she kicked and fought. "Stop fighting. I was told to bring you. It can be dead or alive. If I have to kill you I will make it slow and as painful as possible. You will scream for me to let you die."

Of course, he would. He was just like the others who'd taken her. They hated her because she was an American and a woman. In their eyes, she wasn't sure which was worse. Not that it mattered. But she stopped struggling. She had to give Cam a chance to find her.

"You will not fight me." It wasn't a question. It was an order. She wanted to kick him in the balls. Damn, she was so tempted. But as he walked her down the hallway to the elevator an older woman with a little boy passed them. She knew without a doubt if she made any trouble he'd kill them both. Instead, she cooperated, as the hand on her back directed her down the stairwell instead of the elevator.

Again she contemplated an escape, if she shoved him would he fall and give her a chance to get away? It was possible, but then she had no idea how many 'friends' he had waiting for them outside.

"Don't try it. You think I am an amateur?" The ass could read minds. Wonderful, adrenaline raced through her, but how long it would last was another story. If they got her alone, she'd never survive a second time.

Before he pushed open the stairwell door, he looked through the window. He must have had a communications device like the SEALs because he spoke to someone without pulling out a phone, or maybe it was just Bluetooth. Why it mattered she had no idea, except that it gave her something to think about instead of what he'd do to her.

As soon as he pushed open the door, another man grabbed her, also covered in black. He put a black sack over her head so she couldn't see. Then each of them grabbed an arm and dragged her outside and shoved her into the back of some kind of vehicle. They zip-tied her wrists and ankles and slammed the door.

Alone. Restrained. Blindfolded. This was her nightmare. Except this time she wasn't asleep.

Hope that the tracker was on was all that kept her from losing it. If Tex could track her, Cam could find her, as long as he was alive. He had to be. The alternative was not an option. Somehow, she'd managed to hold it together. The roads were rough, and she was banged into the side of the vehicle so many times she'd have bruises. But they were nothing compared to what she imagined was coming.

At some point during the trip, memories she had blocked, came back in living color. For the first time, she remembered every minute of her captivity, every minute of their torture, and she curled into a ball on the floor. Silent tears soaked the hood, as she tried to deal with the memories, knowing the same was waiting for her.

THE LAST FEW HOURS WERE AMAZING. CAM couldn't remember the last time he'd come so many times in one evening. It didn't seem possible at his age, but damn if that woman didn't bewitch him. With his mind full of Miranda, he wasn't watching his surroundings like he should have been. So when he went, he didn't notice the two men off to the left near a white delivery truck.

The truck should have triggered alarm bells, it was Saturday night, and much too late for deliveries. Halo growled, but Cam was so focused on having him do his business so he could get back upstairs to Miranda, he didn't listen.

The distinctive sound of a bullet shot through a silencer was his first indication of trouble. It whizzed past him and hit Halo. The dog went down. Cam went for his gun, but he was too slow.

A second shot struck his shoulder and the force knocked him to his knees. Halo whimpered and tried to get up, as a pool of blood spread across the concrete.

Fuck. He'd put them all in danger. How could he have been so careless? He didn't have a chance to answer his question. One of the men hit him on the back of the head and the world went black.

When he opened his eyes, his first thought was Miranda. Had they gotten to her? As he struggled to get up, he realized he wasn't on the sidewalk, he was in the hospital. Fuck.

Then it all came back, Halo, the gunshots, Miranda. Fuck. Fuck. Fuck. He must have said the last fuck out loud.

"It's okay, well not okay, but you have a smart woman. I don't know how she did it, but she kept her phone with her. Tex has been tracking her. And if one of those fucks was for Halo, he's going to be fine, it wasn't nearly as bad as it looked," Jake said.

"Thank God."

"You've got a nasty knot on your head and you lost a lot of blood, but it was a through and through. Another nice scar to show the lady. They're keeping you overnight for observation. You know how it goes with the concussion thing."

"Yeah and I don't give a fuck. How long was I out?

"About an hour. It's been about two since they took her as best we can tell."

"I'm not staying in here while Miranda is being tortured or worse."

"Easy, kid. That's why the others aren't here. They're following the tracker. The fuckers got about an hour's head start before the police called me. But we'll get them."

"Yeah, we will. Help me get out of here." Jake was just as stubborn as Cam, but he didn't care. Jake wouldn't stay put if it was his woman, and he wasn't about to either. He'd been shot, stabbed, taken shrapnel, and concussed more times than he could remember. He was a fucking SEAL and he was going to rescue his woman.

Cam pushed the bell for the nurse. When she came in, he was already sitting on the edge of the bed. Either she was going to remove the IV or he would.

"What are you doing, Chief Petty Officer?"

"Discharging myself. Can you please remove this IV?"

"But the doctor…"

"Yes, my CO told me. But I need to get out of here. I promise I'll be careful." Like hell, he would, but at that point, he'd say anything to get out of there. He'd pay for it later, but if he lost Miranda it wouldn't matter.

She glanced at Jake and then back and Cam.

"He means it. He'll pull it out himself and then probably bleed to death."

"Fine, but you have to sign an AMA before you can leave."

"I'll sign whatever I need to, as long as it happens now. We have a woman to save." He'd struggled to keep his voice calm and not curse a blue streak, but it was wearing on him. Thankfully, she grabbed her cart and removed the IV and bandaged him up.

"Let me check your shoulder too." He wanted to say don't bother, but she was doing her job.

He nodded and let her check the dressing. "I should change it before you go."

"Will it take long."

"I'll be quick."

"Fine, thank you. Jake, can you see if my clothes are here?"

"You need a new shirt, they cut it off in the ER."

"Fu…dge." He stopped himself when the nurse raised her eyebrows. "Can you try to find a new one?"

"We can get you a set of scrubs."

"Just the shirt will work. Thank you." Jake hunted it down while Cam got his bandage changed. As soon as she was done, he signed the paper at the nurse's station, and they were out the door.

"You should have stayed overnight. But I wouldn't have either."

"Where is Halo?"

"At the Vet on base. They told me he'd be fine."

"It's all my fault."

"What the fuck are you talking about?"

"I should have been more focused. They never should have gotten the drop on me."

"From what the guy saw who called the police, there were three of them, and they were waiting."

"But if I hadn't been distracted…"

"Shut the fuck up and listen to me. It doesn't matter. It's done. You can beat yourself up later, but I'm telling you, it would have been the same outcome for any of us. You were alone."

"I had Halo."

"Yes but you still couldn't have taken out three with a handgun against three machine guns."

Cam calmed a little as Jake's words sank in. Maybe he couldn't but he'd have gone down fighting, instead of being taken out the way he was. But he was right about one thing, it didn't matter now. Only Miranda mattered.

"Did Tex ever find out where Azfaar is hiding out?"

"Yeah. He called just before I got the call from the police. He's in Syria."

"What the fuck is he doing there?"

"Hiding out with the remaining ISIS fighters."

"He's been working all this long distance?"

"Yup. Seems there are a few cells waiting to be activated. Hopefully, Chrissy can dig up more when she gets the DNA back from the fabric."

"I'm so glad I told Miranda about the tracker and that she found a way to take it with her."

"No shit. Her purse was still at the apartment. They shot through the lock to get in. It didn't look like there was a struggle."

"She was in the shower when I took Halo out for the walk."

"The captain called her father. They're keeping it out of the news for now. No one wants it to get out if we can help it."

"I bet he was fucking thrilled."

"You got that right. He was ready to go to POTUS again. Like what the hell could he do?"

"Activate the FBI. Did he?"

"No. The captain talked him down, but don't be surprised if he shows up here tomorrow."

"That's okay, we'll have her back by then." Cam was positive they would find her and bring her home alive. He had to be. No other outcome was acceptable.

CHAPTER 17

BY THE TIME THEY STOPPED, MIRANDA WAS sore, bruised, scared shitless, and determined not to allow them to hurt her like last time. After reliving every moment of her treatment at the hands of the Taliban last time, she would not give in easily. There was a reason she'd taken all those self-defense classes and now was the time to see if they worked.

Not knowing if Cam was alive or dead didn't help. What if they'd taken him too? Would Tex know to check where she was? The rest of the team wouldn't look for them until tomorrow sometime. Or maybe it was today already.

If there was one thing she was thankful for at that moment, it was that she'd told Cam she loved him. If she was going to die, it was important that he knew what was in her heart, and she knew what was in his. As she focused on the memory of his face when he said the words, the doors were thrown open and a disgusting stench filled her nostrils. Fish? Death? It was horrible and she gagged.

"You'll get used to it, bitch, if you last long enough." This voice was different, not the same accent as at the apartment. This was an American. Hopefully, she'd live long enough to tell Chrissy she was right about the terrorist cell.

Holding on tight to her anger, she was determined to get through this or die trying. Everyone had faith in Tex, so sent him messages, praying that he'd find her and send the team to the rescue.

"Come on," he said as he dragged her from the vehicle by her feet and dropped her on the ground. "Get up."

What an asshat, and what she would give to see his face when someone put a bullet in his brain. Too bad it wouldn't be her. As she struggled to stand, he grabbed her by the upper arm and pulled her to her feet. Then he dragged her along and she struggled to stay upright. With no idea where she was, and unable to see anything, the only clue to her location was the awful smell. As he pulled her along it got stronger.

The ground felt like small pebbles under her feet and she tried to imagine where that would be. Then he stopped. There was a squeal of a metal door, and then a blast of heat like you get when you opened a closed box that's been out in the sun too long. He shoved her inside and slammed the door.

"Hello?" But there was no answer. Reaching out with her tied hands she shuffled forward until she reached a wall. Or maybe it was the door. He'd locked her inside something, and she was alone. Reaching up, she pulled off the hood. It wasn't all that different and still pitch black, but at least she could breathe easier without it.

As she felt along the walls, she got a sinking feeling that she was in a shipping container. How would Cam find her now? Picturing a dock loaded with shipping containers, thousands of them all lined up in rows. Trying to find her would be like searching for a needle in a haystack. She banged on the wall, but all it did was hurt her hands. No answering sound came from outside. Even if someone was around, they wouldn't hear any sounds she made inside.

Terrified, hot and thirsty, she wondered if they planned on leaving her to die in there. Were they going to put it on a ship and send her somewhere? How would anyone find her? She doubted the tracker would work inside the metal box. But she could check. Why hadn't she thought about that sooner?

"Because you were paralyzed with fear and

anger, stupid." Hearing her own voice helped settle her down. She could do this, and if they came back for her, she'd try to get away. She should have tried to get away at the apartment, but the gun had freaked her out. No move she'd learned was any match for a gun.

Why had they left her bound if she was alone? Maybe they were coming back? Or maybe they were just assholes. Her mother would never forgive her for being taken again. She didn't envy whoever drew the short straw and got to tell her. That would not be a pleasant conversation. It almost made her giggle, almost. Then she heard a sound outside. Was someone there?

Pounding the walls with all her strength, she hoped they'd hear her. Over and over she banged on the metal walls. Pain vibrated in her hands and the zip-tie sliced into her wrists. "Please, can you hear me? Help. I'm locked in here."

When the door slid open she had a moment of hope. But it dissipated as fast as it appeared. "No one can hear you. Why bother? Even if they could, they'd never figure out which container you're in."

That's what she'd been afraid of. She recognized the voice. It was the man who'd taken her from the apartment. He pointed a flashlight at her and she was blinded by the bright light after the dense darkness. It was probably better that way.

"Bring the chair, put it there." It figured that he wasn't alone and being bound up she couldn't do much of anything. So far, they hadn't hurt her, but she didn't know how much longer her luck would hold out.

"Grab the girl and put her in the chair."

"Should we put the hood back on?" It was the American. Interesting, so the other guy was in charge. She wished she could see their faces so she could identify them if she made it out of this mess.

"No, we need proof of life." They were going to ransom her again? Didn't they remember how it went the last time? Or was it just a ruse?

The American put Miranda in the chair with a newspaper held against her chest. After a few photos with the paper and a few without, the American dumped her on the floor and took the chair.

"Can you cut me loose? I'm in a freaking box, where am I going to go? And can I have some water?"

"Don't push your luck. Go ahead, cut her loose. But if you try to escape, you'll die. I told you, I don't care if you're alive or dead, but I will have fun cutting you into pieces."

Just the thought of being carved up again made her shiver. He saw her movement and laughed. Where did they find these guys? Did they advertise for cruel sadists with knives who want jihad?

"You're just going to leave me here?"

"For now." And that was it, he backed up and the door slammed shut. Then she heard the latch click into place.

Rubbing her ankles to bring the feeling back, at least they weren't bleeding. But her wrists were a mess. Even without being able to see them, she could feel the stickiness of the blood and the smell of it permeated the stale air of the container.

Reaching under her shirt and into her bra, she dug out her phone. Then pushed the button to check to see if she had a signal. It still had sixty percent battery left but no signal at all. She shouldn't have been surprised since she was in a big metal box.

She turned on the flashlight to check her wrists and see if there was anything in the container she could use as a weapon. But found nothing. Afraid to leave the light on for long and drain the battery, she checked her wrists again. They were chaffed and bloody. She tried to rip part of her shirt to wrap them. Holding the phone in her mouth so she could see, she tried to tear off the bottom of her shirt.

Then she heard the latch, just before the door was opened. She tried to hide the phone but wasn't fast enough. The man grabbed the phone and checked to see if she'd called anyone. Then he punched her with such force, she slammed against the wall and slid onto the floor. Then he kicked her in the ribs.

"You're a sneaky bitch, aren't you? Ishmael will not be happy. Here he took pity on you and sent me to bring you water. Where did you have this hiding?"

Miranda didn't say anything as tears slid down her cheeks. It was her one lifeline and she'd lost it.

"What's going on?"

"I found this, the bitch had it when I opened the door."

"Where did you have it? I should have kept you naked. It would have been harder to hide anything. Strip her down."

"No. I don't have anything else."

"I warned you. You didn't listen."

The American pulled her to her feet, and she kicked him in the balls. They might kill her, but she wasn't going to make it easy for them.

"You fucking cunt, you're going to pay for that." He punched her in the head, and she crumpled like a rag doll.

~

JAKE'S PHONE RANG, AND HE HIT THE ANSWER button in the truck. It was Rafe.

"We lost the signal about twenty minutes ago. Tex hasn't been able to get it back."

"Where did it drop?"

"At the Port."

"Fuck. She could be anywhere."

"No, she'd have to be someplace that blocked the signal, unless the phone went dead."

"We're about ten minutes away. Where are you?"

"Outside the custom's terminal."

"Copy that."

Cam wanted to put his fist through the dashboard he was so frustrated. They'd had his Sunshine for too long and worried what they'd done to her.

"We'll find her. But, dammit Cam, you need to focus. Detach yourself from the personal stuff or you're going to go off half-cocked and get yourself or one of us killed. That's an order."

Jake was right. This wasn't him. He'd busted his ass to make spec ops. This was another mission. He'd keep repeating it in his head until he believed it. When Cam had her in his arms, then it could be personal. Clearing his head with a shake, he focused on the end game. Rescuing Miranda and taking out the tangos.

"Copy that."

Jake shut off his lights as he pulled in next to

Rafe's truck and turned off the ignition. "Are you ready?"

"Yes, Boss. I wish we had Halo."

"Me too. Hell, I'm sure he'd like to get a piece of them too."

"Yeah."

"Put this on." He tossed him a black t-shirt he'd dug out of his go bag, then handed him a night vision helmet.

"Thanks." Cam changed shirts, being careful not to rip off the dressing on his shoulder and then put on the helmet.

"How's the shoulder?"

"Perfect." Jake grinned, flashing white teeth in the darkness.

"Let's go get Miranda and end these fuckers."

"Copy that, Boss."

Murph was waiting for them in the shadows at the edge of the customs terminal.

"Sitrep?"

"Eagle 2 and 3 are on recon. Tex messaged that the tracker turned on for a moment then went dark."

"Copy that."

"What are we waiting for?" Cam asked impatiently.

"For Eagle 2 and 3 to return. Or report in."

He hated waiting which was one of the reasons he'd been happy to train to be the K-9 operator. He and Halo always took point. No waiting.

"Eagle 2, this is Eagle 1, sitrep."

"Eagle 1, we are about one klick south of your location. We have eyes on two tangos."

"Copy that Eagle 2. Any sign of the HVT?"

"Negative, Eagle 1."

"Copy that. We're coming to you." Following Jake, they stayed in the shadows as they navigated to the location of the rest of the team. About a half a klick from where they'd started they reached the fenced off customs containment area. A few moments later, the met up with Rafe and Ryan.

"Anything?"

"Maybe. Two guys just came back from that direction. They're inside the office over there," Rafe said as he pointed to the right. "I'm not sure where they came from."

"Okay, let's see what they do next."

Staying to the shadows, they didn't have to wait long. The door opened and one of the guys came out.

"Stay with him."

"Copy that." Cam wanted to go, but he was a liability with his injury. A few seconds later another guy came out and headed in the same direction.

"Okay, Cam you're with me. Murph, stay here and keep watch."

"Copy that."

They silently followed the second tango. As they rounded the second container, Rafe's voice came over the com. "Eagle 1, we've located HVT."

"Copy that, Eagle 2, status?"

"She's alive."

Relief coursed through Cam's veins, followed by anger at the men who'd dared to take his woman. "Easy, we don't know the whole situation yet."

"Copy that." Jake was right. They reached Rafe and Ryan in time for the second man to walk into an open container.

"She's inside."

"You fucking cunt, you're going to pay for that."

"Go, go, go. Remember, we need them alive," Jake whispered. Rafe was the first one into the container and neutralized the first tango, Ryan got the second. By the time Jake and Cam got through the doorway, it was all over.

"She's there, kid. Easy, this fucktard hit her hard," he said as he kicked him.

Cam couldn't get to her side fast enough. A bruise was already visible on her right cheek and her eye was swollen. It reminded him so much of the last time. Checking for a pulse, it was there, slow but steady. But she was unconscious.

"Ryan, she's not responding."

"Copy that." He checked her vitals. "He hit her hard. I'm sure she has a concussion."

"You're twins now," Murph said as he appeared in the doorway.

"What happened to stay behind and keep watch."

"I got tired of waiting and took out the other two in the shack. They're tied up nice and pretty."

Jake shook his head, but the rest of the team laughed. It was typical Murph.

"We need to get her checked out. How do you want to handle this, Boss?"

"I'll call the captain then he can call the FBI."

"Copy that."

It didn't take long for the FBI to show up along with an ambulance to take Miranda to the hospital. Since Chrissy had already briefed her superiors per the captain's suggestion. It went a lot more smoothly than if they'd involved the police, and they'd share pertinent intel that could help them get their hands on Azfaar.

Cam rode in the ambulance with Miranda. The EMT used smelling salts and it woke her up. He'd never been so happy to see anyone open their eyes.

"Hi, Sunshine."

"Cam. Oh my God. I thought I'd never see you again," she said as she tried to sit up.

"Wow. Hold on there, ma'am. You need to stay still."

"Where are we?"

"In an ambulance on the way to the hospital. That dirtbag hit you fucking hard. You most likely have a concussion." She nodded and closed her eyes. He worried she'd lost consciousness, but she opened her eyes again a moment later.

"I thought you were dead," she said softly as tears filled her eyes.

"I'm so sorry. I shouldn't have left you alone."

"No, it's not your fault."

"If it's okay with you two, can I finish checking her vitals before we get to the hospital?"

"Sorry," Cam said and moved out of the EMTs way but stayed within view of Miranda's eyes to keep them both calm. He owed Tex big time and he had no idea how he'd ever repay him. Miranda would have been gone forever if not for him.

CHAPTER 18

MIRANDA HAD A CONCUSSION, FOUR BROKEN ribs, a swollen eye, a bruised jaw, and her wrists were torn up from being restrained in the zip-ties. As they rolled her gurney into her hospital room, Cam got his first look at her since they'd tossed him out of the ER, and it shredded his heart. Covered in bruises of assorted shades, wrists wrapped in bandages and assorted cuts and scrapes, it was like déjà vu. Would it be better if he got out of her life? It would be safer for her. But could he walk away from her and have anything left?

"Cam? Whatever you're thinking, cut it out."

"What?" She'd opened her eyes and was staring up at him from the hospital bed. "I thought you were sleeping."

"No, just resting my eye."

"How are you, Sunshine? I thought I'd lost you. I'm so sorry. I love you with all of my heart." He ached to hold her, to wrap her in his arms and never let her go. But between the machines, the IV, and her ribs, he hesitated to touch her.

"I thought I'd lost you too. I'm so much better now that I know you're okay. I was so worried about you and Halo. I can't imagine my life without you in it. Where's Halo?"

"He's fine, I promise. He was shot and had to go to the Vet. We can probably pick him up in a day or two. Maybe sooner."

"They shot him? What is wrong with these people?" She struggled to sit up and he rushed to her side.

"Easy, remember your ribs." From her wince, it was obvious that the pain reminded her.

"I can't believe they broke my ribs again. Is it mean guy 101? Go for the face and the ribs?"

"Hmm, maybe. I'll have to look that up in my training information." She giggled, at least it was some combination of giggle and groan, which was the reaction he'd been hoping for, without the pain.

"Cam, you're bleeding. What happened? He followed her eyes to his shoulder. He must have opened the wound at some point and even though he was wearing black the blood was visible.

"Nothing, it's just a scratch. I'm fine."

"I don't believe you. I knew they did something to you to keep you from me. Don't try to tell me it's nothing, or you would have kept me from being taken. I know you."

He couldn't understand how she had such blind faith in him when he'd failed her. "We were ambushed, but I should have been expecting something. If I had..."

"I told you earlier, you and Halo could not have held off three armed men. You're good but you're not that good," Jake said as he walked into the room obviously overhearing Miranda's comment.

"See, even your boss thinks so. Thank you, Jake. If it weren't for you and your team..."

"Most of the credit on this one has to go to Tex. If it wasn't for his tracker I'm not sure we would have found you in time." It's what Cam had been thinking too.

"I'm glad too. I prayed that he'd realize I was in trouble. I wasn't sure what happened to Cam, so I didn't know if anyone would realize I was missing."

"We found out pretty quickly. A witness called the police and they called me after they found Cam and Halo unconscious on the sidewalk."

"Shouldn't you be in the hospital too?"

"No, I'm exactly where I should be. I'll be fine. It's not the first or the last time I'll be hurt on a mission." He carefully avoided the word 'shot' since he didn't want her to worry more than she was already.

"Did you catch Ishmael and the American?"

"Yes, and two others. The FBI has them now. We're hoping that they'll turn on each other. It all depends if they are true jihadists or were just in it for the money."

"They were going to demand a ransom. They took pictures of me with a newspaper."

Cam and Jake exchanged looks. Interesting, maybe this was another piece of the puzzle. They'd figured out most of it.

Some of it still didn't add up. Like why not kill him when they could have? Why try to ransom Miranda again? Were there two different plans, with different people behind them? With so many unanswered questions, they hoped at least one of them would flip on the others. From what Chrissy had told Jake, none of them had said a word.

"Speaking of ransom, your father should be here soon. The FBI contacted him when you were rescued. And before you ask, no, I don't think your mom knows."

"Thank God. It is bad enough Dad knows. But if Mom found out she'd build a dungeon and lock me up to keep me safe."

Jake laughed but Cam knew she was serious. He'd met Cherise Stanhope, and nothing was more important than keeping her family safe. When she found out, and he had no doubt she would, he'd be persona non grata.

"I'm sorry, Miranda. You never should have been involved this time."

"I think I was involved since they realized I was here. It sucks, yes. But hopefully, it is done now." Cam would have loved to tell her it was, but Azfaar was still out there somewhere and until they caught him it wouldn't be over for any of them.

"How's your head, Sunshine? Do you need anything for pain?" he asked as she shifted in the bed and groaned.

"No, I don't want anything. My head hurts a bit, but the ribs are worse. Luckily I know how long I'll feel like this." She smiled tremulously. "Is everyone else safe? No one else was hurt, right?"

"Everyone is good. The guys are waiting outside, we didn't want to crowd you all at once."

"Dang, tell them to come in. I need to thank all of you. And Tex too."

"We can take care of that. Tomorrow we'll give him a call and you can talk to him."

"That would be great." Jake went out to the waiting room to get the others and Cam sat on the edge of the bed, hoping he wouldn't cause her any additional pain.

"Are you afraid of me?"

"No, of course not, just afraid of hurting you, Sunshine. You've been through hell again."

"This time was a piece of cake. When they took me, then put a hood over my head and threw me in the back of the vehicle, all my memories came flooding back. I know why I'm having the nightmares. It's because of what I tried to forget."

Before she could tell him, Jake was back with Rafe, Ryan, and Murph. The only one missing was Halo, and he hoped he was okay. After four years of having him constantly at his side, he was lost without his furry sidekick.

"We'll talk later. Okay?" he whispered as he kissed her softly on the lips.

"Okay."

"You look pretty good considering," Murph announced.

"Gee thanks, I appreciate that Murph. You don't look too bad yourself, considering," Miranda answered and the expression on Murph's face made them all laugh. It also reassured him that she wasn't as bad off as he'd thought, not if she was making jokes already.

"I didn't mean it that way," Murph mumbled and looked embarrassed.

"I know. I was just playing along. Seriously, you guys are amazing. I feel like I have my own personal SEAL team."

"I doubt Uncle Sam would want to hear that.

And we didn't *do* anything. Just helped out a friend who was in trouble," Jake answered for the team and the others nodded. They weren't allowed to operate on home soil, and they were hoping to keep the whole thing quiet.

"I'm sure he wouldn't be too happy," a voice replied from the doorway. Cam turned around and stared into the hard angry blue eyes of Senator Richard Stanhope.

"Daddy," Miranda screeched when she heard her father's voice. The SEALs made room for him and Cam stood up and moved away from the bed. When Stanhope turned his eyes to his daughter they softened, and he smiled.

"How are you, baby girl?"

"I'm fine. Really. And you need to be nicer to them. They've saved me twice now."

"Yes, they have, but I'm not sure why this time happened."

"Neither are we, Sir," Jake answered. "But we'll be happy to tell you what we know."

"Thank you for saving my daughter. And yes, I'll want a full report."

"How about we let you and your dad have some time. We'll be right down the hall, Sunshine," Cam said, hoping that the man would calm down when he realized she would make a full recovery.

Miranda nodded and mouthed a thank you, as

her father shook Jake's hand. "Call if you need me."

~

"SUNSHINE? IS THAT WHAT HE CALLS YOU?" Richard Stanhope asked as he pulled a chair over to the side of Miranda's bed.

"Yes. I think it's sweet."

"How are you? The doctor gave me an update, but just because it says something on paper it doesn't give you the whole picture."

"I'm okay. Just like the doctor told you. Nothing life threatening, just a few broken ribs, and lots of bruises and scratches."

"How did you get involved in this mess?"

"I don't know. But it's the same group as in Afghanistan."

"Didn't the SEALs take them out?"

"Yes, but you know how it goes, cut off the head of the snake and two grow back."

"This isn't an action movie, Miranda, this is real life. I don't want to have to worry about my daughter every time she leaves the house."

"You don't"

"That's not true. I think you should come home with me when they discharge you."

"No."

"No? What do you mean no?"

"I'm not going with you. I'll fly back next week like I'm supposed to."

"Why are you being so stubborn? Don't you want Mom to take care of you?"

"No. I'm sorry, Daddy, but I'm almost twenty-six years old. You need to let me live my life. Why do you think I joined the missionary group? Yes, I wanted to help, but it was the only way I could get away without you guys flipping out."

As her father listened to her, emotions spread across his face. Anger, shock, and as her words sank in, resignation. He'd never considered that she'd grown up.

"Is that how you really feel?" Her heart ached as he seemed to age before her eyes.

"Yes, it is. It's not that I don't love you both. I do. But I need to live the life I want, just like you did."

"I'm sorry if you felt that you couldn't."

"It's okay, I should have spoken up sooner. Until all of that happened in Afghanistan I don't think I realized it. But while I was stuck in that cave and convinced I was going to die, it made me think about how much I still wanted to do with my life."

Stanhope nodded. "Do you want me to talk to your mother?"

"No, I will when I come home. But you should know, I'm planning on moving here."

"To live with the SEAL?"

"Yes, but that's not the reason. I have friends here, real friends for the first time in my life. I've had more fun in the last three days than I can remember."

"You have friends in Atlanta, what about Barbara Jean? And Crystal?"

"They were okay, but they were mom approved, and we never did anything. Seriously, it's okay. I don't blame anyone. It was the life we had. I love you. But it's time to let me go."

"DC isn't far from here, will you come to visit?"

"Of course, I will, and to Atlanta too. It's not like I'm moving to Europe."

"Thank God for small favors," he said. Miranda laughed. It was a huge weight off of her shoulders when she told him. It had been stupid to wait so long, but it was done now. Or would be after she explained it to her mom. That would be harder.

"Will this SEAL take care of you like he should?"

"The SEAL's name is Cam. And we'll take care of each other. He's an amazing person, you'll realize it when you get to know him better."

"We'll see."

"I know you already had him checked out. I'm your daughter, remember?"

Stanhope smiled. "Yes, you are. And you will always be my baby girl."

"I know, Daddy. Now give me a kiss and then you can go back to work."

"So this is how it's going to be now?"

"Yup," Miranda said with a big smile on her bruised face.

"You know, with those bruises that smile is kind of creepy."

"Really?"

"No. Well maybe," he joked then dropped a kiss on her forehead. "I love you. I'm only a phone call away."

"I know. I'll call you when I break out of here."

"Oh God, he's rubbing off on you already." It was true, and Miranda grinned.

"Bye, Daddy."

The SEALs were down the hall in the waiting room and Stanhope stopped in.

"You're Cameron Patterson, right?

"Yes, Sir." Stanhope reached for his hand and shook it.

"Take good care of her or I'll find out about it."

"Yes, Sir."

Then he turned and walked to the elevator. When the doors opened he stepped inside and nodded at Cam as the doors slid shut.

"I'M GOING TO STAY WITH HER TONIGHT. DO you think one of you can get the door fixed for me?"

"Yeah, no problem, I'll work on it," Murph said. "Do you care what kind of lock I put on?"

"Nope, as long as it's bulletproof." He'd meant it as a joke, but he didn't quite pull it off. "Seriously, anything is fine. But this way I can bring Miranda and hopefully Halo home tomorrow."

"You got it. If you need anything else, let us know," Jake said.

"Say goodbye to Miranda for us. Don't be surprised if Meghan calls her later. Oh, that reminds me. Here's a new phone for her, and yes, it has a tracker. I had a few spares from Meghan's trip."

"Great, thank you. I'll get it programmed for her and she'll be ready for Meghan later."

Cam peeked into Miranda's room to make sure she wasn't sleeping.

"I'm awake."

"I see that. How did it go with your father? He stopped by and told me to take good care of you."

"He did? I guess I shouldn't be surprised. I told him I was moving here."

"Fuck. And you didn't warn me?" Cam said with a laugh.

"Don't worry, I explained it to him. I think he'll be fine. But I can't promise he won't drop in from time-to-time."

"That doesn't bother me. They can come as often as they want."

"Thank you."

He leaned down and kissed her. The need to touch her, to reassure himself that she was okay was overpowering. "I love you."

"I love you. Did the guys leave?"

"Yeah. I figured you'd want to talk. Was I wrong?"

"No, you were right." She scooted over on the bed. "And after we get settled, I'm going to see the therapist Meghan recommended."

"That's great, I think it will be good for you. I know she helped her a lot."

"Yeah. I should have listened to everyone months ago. I guess in some ways I'm my father's daughter. Think you'll be able to put up with me?"

Cam laughed. "Of course. You can't get rid of me that easily. And I mean it. You can't do or say anything to make me love you any less. So whatever it is you're about to say, you don't have to worry."

Miranda nodded, and then took a deep breath which made her wince. But Cam didn't say anything. Just sat next to her and held her hand gently.

"Okay, I hope you're right. I have never been ashamed of my body, I was happy with it the way it was, not perfect, but me." He nodded in encouragement.

"But after Afghanistan, I kept trying to hide it, especially my legs because of the scars. I couldn't remember how I'd gotten them until tonight then it all came back. They screamed foul things, called me an infidel and so many words I didn't understand. Over and over, and each time they'd cut me. I was so sure I was going to die, cut to ribbons, blood everywhere and it hurt so much."

Tears slid down her cheeks and he ached for her. His gut twisting into knots. Anger swept through him with such force he thought he'd explode. He vowed then and there that Azfaar would pay for what he'd done to Miranda, and he'd be screaming for death long before Cam let him take his last breath.

No wonder she'd been so traumatized. Her bravery astounded him even now, and he couldn't have been more impressed that she'd come so far without help. Every so gently he slid one arm underneath her and hugged her. He would give anything to take away the memories, the pain, but it wasn't in his power. But he could support her, be there as she worked through all of it.

"You survived it and came out the other side. It's all that's important, and what you need to hold on to. I know the doctor will help you, but I couldn't love you more than I do right now. You have been through so much, you're so brave, and beautiful. Those scars don't define you. They're part of your history, proof of what you've overcome."

"You not disgusted?"

"How could I be? None of it was your fault. You survived so I could find you and love you for the rest of our lives."

"How did I get so lucky?"

"I ask myself the same question all the time."

"Thank you for everything."

"Miranda, you don't have to thank me, just love me."

"Always."

EPILOGUE

Three months later…

"That's the last of them," Cam said as he dropped the box on the floor of the apartment that he now officially shared with Miranda and Halo. He had no doubt that Halo was just as happy to have her there. He hadn't left her side from the moment he'd seen her at the airport. They'd rented a U-Haul to move her stuff from her parent's house in Atlanta, and damn there had been a lot of stuff.

"That's all of them?" Halo barked.

"Yes, isn't it enough? Just how many freakin' book boxes were there?"

"You're lucky I didn't bring them all. I left plenty behind."

"I guess I'm going to have to put shelves up in the spare bedroom."

"Probably in here too," she said as she looked around. "Hmm, maybe our bedroom too." Then she burst into a fit of giggles. God, it was good to hear her laugh, and now he'd hear it every day.

"They warned me that you'd take over. You even stole my dog."

"What? How could I steal your dog?" As she reached down to pet Halo, who was sitting by her side. He'd fully recovered and had been cleared for missions again. But thankfully, they hadn't had one yet.

"Yes, look at him sitting there."

"Me? Steal your dog? Never. And take over? Well, bless their little hearts." Now it was Cam's turn to laugh.

"Where do you want to start?" Cam asked as he looked around at the piles of boxes. Most of them were books and he'd have to stack them in the spare room for now.

"I was thinking in the bedroom."

"Oh okay, let me grab a couple of boxes and I'll meet you there."

"Umm, no boxes, just you. I've waited long enough. My ribs are healed, and I want you."

"Well if you put it like that." Cam lifted her into his arms and carried her into their bedroom.

He liked the sound of that. Halo was right by his side.

"Halo, boy, I'm afraid you're going to have to stay on the other side of the door." The dog looked dejected, but he had to draw the line someplace. Then he dropped Miranda gently onto the bed.

"I love you, Cam. You and that wonderful dog are the best knights in shining armor ever."

"And I love you, Sunshine. You are truly the light of my life just like the fortune predicted."

The End

ABOUT THE AUTHOR

Lynne St. James has been writing for as long as she can remember. She has series in romantic suspense, contemporary, new adult and paranormal. She lives in the mostly sunny state of Florida with her husband, an eighty-five-pound, fluffy, Dalmatian-mutt horse-dog, a small Yorkie-poo, and an orange tabby named Pumpkin who thinks he rules them all.

When Lynne's not writing about second chances and conquering adversity with happily ever afters, she's drinking coffee and reading or crocheting.

Where to find Lynne:

Email: lynne@lynnestjames.com
Amazon: https://amzn.to/2sgdUTe
BookBub: https://www.bookbub.com/authors/lynne-st-james
Facebook: https://www.facebook.com/authorLynneStJames
Website: http://lynnestjames.com

Instagram: https://www.
instagram.com/lynnestjames/
Pinterest: https://www.
pinterest.com/lynnestjames5
VIP Newsletter sign-up: http://
eepurl.com/bT99Fj

facebook.com/authorLynneStJames
twitter.com/lynnestjames
instagram.com/lynnestjames
bookbub.com/authors/lynne-st-james

BOOKS BY LYNNE ST. JAMES

Beyond Valor

A Soldier's Gift, Book 1

A Soldier's Forever, Book 2

A Soldier's Triumph, Book 3

A Soldier's Protection, Book 4

A Soldier's Pledge, Book 5

A Soldier's Destiny, Book 6

A Soldier's Homecoming, Book 7 (coming soon)

A Soldier's Redemption, Book 8 (coming Soon)

Black Eagle Team

SEAL's Spitfire: Special Forces: Operation Alpha, Book 1

SEAL's Sunshine: Special Forces: Operation Alpha, Book 2

Raining Chaos

Taming Chaos, Book 1

Seducing Wrath, Book 2

Music under the Mistletoe – A Raining Chaos Christmas
(Novella) Book 2.5

Tempting Flame, Book 3

Anamchara

Embracing Her Desires, Book 1

Embracing Her Surrender, Book 2

Embracing Her Love, Book 3

The Vampires of Eternity

Twice Bitten Not Shy

Twice Bitten to Paradise

Twice Bitten and Bewitched

Want to be one of the first to learn about Lynne St. James's new releases? Sign up for her newsletter filled with exclusive VIP news and contests! http://eepurl.com/bT99Fj

There are many more books in this fan fiction world than listed here, for an up-to-date list go to www.AcesPress.com

You can also visit our Amazon page at: http://www.amazon.com/author/operationalpha

Special Forces: Operation Alpha World

Denise Agnew: Dangerous to Hold
Shauna Allen: Awakening Aubrey
Shauna Allen: Defending Danielle
Shauna Allen: Rescuing Rebekah
Shauna Allen: Saving Scarlett
Shauna Allen: Saving Grace
Brynne Asher: Blackburn
Jennifer Becker: Hiding Catherine
Julia Bright: Saving Lorelei
Julia Bright: Rescuing Amy
Victoria Bright: Surviving Savage
Victoria Bright: Going Ghost
Victoria Bright: Jostling Joker
Cara Carnes: Protecting Mari
Kendra Mei Chailyn: Beast
Kendra Mei Chailyn: Barbie
Kendra Mei Chailyn : Pitbull
Melissa Kay Clarke: Rescuing Annabeth
Melissa Kay Clarke: Safeguarding Miley
Samantha A. Cole: Handling Haven
Samantha A. Cole: Cheating the Devil

Sue Coletta: Hacked
Melissa Combs: Gallant
KaLyn Cooper: Rescuing Melina
Liz Crowe: Marking Mariah
Jordan Dane: Redemption for Avery
Jordan Dane: Fiona's Salvation
Riley Edwards: Protecting Olivia
Riley Edwards: Redeeming Violet
Riley Edwards, Recovering Ivy
Nicole Flockton: Protecting Maria
Nicole Flockton: Guarding Erin
Nicole Flockton: Guarding Suzie
Nicole Flockton: Guarding Brielle
Casey Hagen: Shielding Nebraska
Casey Hagen: Shielding Harlow
Casey Hagen: Shielding Josie
Casey Hagen: Shielding Blair
Desiree Holt: Protecting Maddie
Kathy Ivan: Saving Sarah
Kathy Ivan: Saving Savannah
Kathy Ivan: Saving Stephanie
Jesse Jacobson: Protecting Honor
Jesse Jacobson: Fighting for Honor
Jesse Jacobson: Defending Honor
Jesse Jacobson: Summer Breeze
Silver James: Rescue Moon
Silver James: SEAL Moon
Silver James: Assassin's Moon
Silver James: Under the Assassin's Moon

Becca Jameson: Saving Sofia
Kate Kinsley: Protecting Ava
Heather Long: Securing Arizona
Heather Long: Guarding Gertrude
Heather Long: Protecting Pilar
Heather Long: Covering Coco
Gennita Low: No Protection
Kirsten Lynn: Joining Forces for Jesse
Margaret Madigan: Bang for the Buck
Margaret Madigan: Buck the System
Margaret Madigan: Jungle Buck
Margaret Madigan: December Chill
Rachel McNeely: The SEAL's Surprise Baby
Rachel McNeely: The SEAL's Surprise Bride
Rachel McNeely: The SEAL's Surprise Twin
KD Michaels: Saving Laura
KD Michaels: Protecting Shane
KD Michaels: Avenging Angels
Wren Michaels: The Fox & The Hound
Wren Michaels: The Fox & The Hound 2
Wren Michaels: Shadow of Doubt
Wren Michaels: Shift of Fate
Wren Michaels: Steeling His Heart
Kat Mizera: Protecting Bobbi
Mary B Moore: Force Protection
LeTeisha Newton: Protecting Butterfly
LeTeisha Newton: Protecting Goddess
LeTeisha Newton: Protecting Vixen
LeTeisha Newton: Protecting Heartbeat

MJ Nightingale: Protecting Beauty
MJ Nightingale: Betting on Benny
MJ Nightingale: Protecting Secrets
Sarah O'Rourke: Saving Liberty
Debra Parmley: Protecting Pippa
Lainey Reese: Protecting New York
Jenika Snow: Protecting Lily
Jen Talty: Burning Desire
Jen Talty: Burning Kiss
Jen Talty: Burning Skies
Jen Talty: Burning Lies
Jen Talty: Burning Heart
Megan Vernon: Protecting Us
Megan Vernon: Protecting Earth

Police and Fire: Operation Alpha World

Freya Barker: Burning for Autumn
KaLyn Cooper: Justice for Gwen
Aspen Drake: Sheltering Emma
Deanndra Hall: Shelter for Sharla
Deanndra Hall:Justice for Aleta
Barb Han: Kace
Reina Torres: Justice for Sloane
Stacey Wilk: Stage Fright

As you know, this book included at least one character from Susan Stoker's books. To check out more, see below.

SEAL of Protection: Legacy Series

Securing Caite

Securing Brenae (novella)

Securing Sidney

Securing Piper (Aug 2019)

Securing Zoey (Jan 2020)

Securing Avery (May 2020)

Securing Kalee (Sept 2020)

Delta Force Heroes Series

Rescuing Rayne (FREE!)

Rescuing Aimee (novella)

Rescuing Emily

Rescuing Harley

Marrying Emily (novella)

Rescuing Kassie

Rescuing Bryn

Rescuing Casey

Rescuing Sadie (novella)

Rescuing Wendy

Rescuing Mary

Rescuing Macie (Novella)

Badge of Honor: Texas Heroes Series

Justice for Mackenzie (FREE!)
Justice for Mickie
Justice for Corrie
Justice for Laine (novella)
Shelter for Elizabeth
Justice for Boone
Shelter for Adeline
Shelter for Sophie
Justice for Erin
Justice for Milena
Shelter for Blythe
Justice for Hope
Shelter for Quinn
Shelter for Koren (July 2019)
Shelter for Penelope (Oct 2019)

SEAL of Protection Series

Protecting Caroline (FREE!)
Protecting Alabama
Protecting Fiona
Marrying Caroline (novella)
Protecting Summer
Protecting Cheyenne
Protecting Jessyka
Protecting Julie (novella)
Protecting Melody
Protecting the Future
Protecting Kiera (novella)
Protecting Alabama's Kids (novella)

Protecting Dakota

New York Times, *USA Today* and *Wall Street Journal* Bestselling Author Susan Stoker has a heart as big as the state of Tennessee where she lives, but this all American girl has also spent the last fourteen years living in Missouri, California, Colorado, Indiana, and Texas. She's married to a retired Army man who now gets to follow *her* around the country.

She debuted her first series in 2014 and quickly followed that up with the SEAL of Protection Series, which solidified her love of writing and creating stories readers can get lost in.

If you enjoyed this book, or any book, please consider leaving a review. It's appreciated by authors more than you'll know.

www.stokeraces.com
www.AcesPress.com
susan@stokeraces.com

Made in the USA
Monee, IL
10 March 2020

23007710R00148